Haunted Regression

B Gibbins

Published under licence by The Self-Publishing Partnership,
7 Green Park Station, Bath BA1 1JB

www.selfpublishingpartnership.co.uk

ISBN printed book: 978-1-83952-237-6

Cover design by Leigh Lovett
Internal design by Andrew Easton

This book is printed on FSC certified paper

Printed and bound in the UK

Haunted Regression

By Colin Gibbins

Overlooking the cove on the outskirts of the old Cornish town of Porthleven stood The Old Lugger Inn. The three-hundred-year-old Inn, once used by Smugglers, was now a popular meeting place for locals and tourists. Steeped in history and untouched, it was still in its original state with stone walls and floors, and huge timber beams, which helped to create a charmed, mysterious atmosphere.

Music could be heard from an open window and in the corner of the quaint, dingy, smoke-filled bar sat a young boy and three old fishermen. The fishermen were dressed in big, sloppy, polo-necked jumpers, baggy pants tucked into their wellington boots and old battered hats; their hair was white as snow, as were their unkempt, bushy beards. One of them, Henry Channon, who was the father of the Inn owner, played the concertina and the other two fishermen, slumped back in their seats holding grubby clay pipes, sang along to the old sea shanties. The young boy Harry Channon, Henry's grandson, joined in with the singing, along with the room full of tourists and the regulars while his mother and father, Mary and John, served drinks behind the bar.

All of a sudden, the music stopped. The room subsided into a still, eerie silence as John dimmed the lights and Henry put down his concertina and lit up his clay pipe. He started to tell his story of the history of the Inn, his weather-beaten, craggy face etched with passion and verve, his croaky voice hollow and haunting. The regulars had heard the story many times but the tourists held their breath, dwelling on his every word as he talked of smugglers, wreckers and pirates. He told of the Inn being the meeting place of the smugglers and how the spirits of his ancestors, who were part of that community still to this day, resided at the Inn.

Harry sat close by, soaking up every word, totally engrossed. His father, John, blamed those stories for the terrifying, haunted nightmares Harry had experienced over the years and tried to discourage them from spending so much time together. But Harry was somehow drawn to his grandfather and spent every spare hour in his company.

Henry finished his story, tuned up his concertina and the room broke out into another sea shanty.

After school each day, Harry would jump off the bus and race up the hill, his mop of black, curly hair flowing in the breeze. As he reached the Inn at the top, he would throw his school bag into the passage before scuttling round the back, where his grandfather was working in a large wooden workshop, restoring an old boat. The sea and boats were in the Channon blood and like the generations gone before Harry was eager to learn the art of boat building and maintenance. His grandfather had the time and inclination to make sure all of his knowledge and experience was passed down to his beloved grandson.

Henry took Harry through every step of the operation, patiently guiding and prompting, and allowing Harry to use his treasured tools to slowly strip down the old boat and build it back up again, while renewing the worn and damaged parts.

John stuck his head round the door. 'Have you no young friends you want to spend time with?' he said shaking his head. 'It's not healthy. Your mother is worried too, and you,' he said turning to Henry, 'you should have more sense. Do you have to tell the lad these far-fetched tales?'

'Tales!' Henry said indignantly. 'They are not tales! They are Cornish folklore passed down through generations in the Channon household.'

They were interrupted by the sound of Mary's voice calling them in for tea. Henry put down his tools and slipped his arm around Harry's shoulder, ushering him out of the workshop; he glanced back at John with an icy glare.

Most weekends Harry and his grandfather would sail out of the harbour in Penzance on Henry's boat, dressed as pirates and flying the Jolly Roger flag. They travelled around the coast, visiting the beautiful coves, exploring the many smugglers' caves in search of hidden booty. What with all the old stories and these adventures it was little wonder that Harry believed Henry when he told him they had both been pirates in a past life.

It was no surprise that when Harry left school, he went to work at the boatyard in Penzance to learn the craft of boat building. He used his father's rigid inflatable dinghy as transport. The dinghy was moored in a small boathouse down the bank from the Inn. It was fitted with an outboard motor to ensure a speedy journey along the coast to the boatyard inside Penzance harbour.

The time he had spent with his grandfather stood him in good stead and he soon became an important part of the team.

The owner of the yard, Mike Williams, followed his progress with interest and took a shine to this new hard-working, happy-go-lucky young man.

One day, shortly after finishing his apprenticeship, Harry arrived at the yard, tied up his dinghy and made his way up towards the workshop. Bill, the foreman, called Harry over to inform him that Mr Williams would like to speak to him in his office. Harry looked uncomfortable. As he made his way tentatively along the passage, he paused a moment outside the office door to collect his thoughts. Maybe now he was entitled to full pay they would get rid of him or maybe he had messed up the boat they were busy working on; his mind was racing nineteen to the dozen. Only one way to find out. He wiped his brow with his handkerchief, dusted down his top, took a deep breath and knocked gently on the door.

As he stood patiently for a few moments, he could hear voices inside but the wait seemed to go on and on. He started to sweat a little and just managed to mop his brow before the door finally opened. The office secretary beckoned him inside and ushered him over to a chair in front of Mr Williams' desk. Harry remained standing as Mr Williams closed a file he was working on and slipped it into a drawer. A big, warm smile crossed his face as he sank back into his chair.

'Please sit down and relax; you're not in any trouble. I just wanted to congratulate you on completing your apprenticeship and wondered if you are happy to continue working with us.'

'Of course,' said Harry with a sigh of relief. 'My whole life has revolved and does revolve around boats and sailing – a Channon tradition.'

Mike nodded his head in approval. 'That's good news. As you know, I have been competing in the cross-channel races with little success, so I am looking to extend the design team to improve my chances of winning a major trophy. If you are interested, I will make arrangements for you to attend college to gain qualifications in boat building and design. You will continue to work with the boat-building team at the yard and sit in on sessions with the design team to gain experience.'

Harry shook his head in disbelief. 'Design team! How wonderful! Thank you so much! I will work so hard to make sure your faith is rewarded.' They shook hands and Harry floated out of the office on the crest of a wave.

Over the following weeks Harry continued working on Mike's new boat, 'The French Connection'. His pending promotion had given him an extra incentive and time spent with his grandfather was now dedicated to Mike's team. Although Henry missed their quality time together, he understood, and encouraged Harry to follow his dream. He was so proud and felt he could take part of the credit with all the training and knowledge he had passed on over the years.

Come the day of the race, a large crowd had gathered on the promenade of Penzance Harbour. Harry, John and Henry arrived early and were standing at the front. Harry was so proud and excited; although he had watched many of the races, this time was different – he was part of the team that had built the boat and he felt entitled to share the whole experience.

There were several mobile shops selling refreshments as the crowd waited patiently for sight of the boats through the morning and into the afternoon. The sun was warm and a gentle breeze nudged small, fluffy, white clouds rolling across the sky above them. Suddenly there was an outburst of cheering as the first boat appeared on the distant horizon. Harry was so excited as he fumbled in his bag for his binoculars. A tannoy nearby informed them that several of the race leaders were in close contention.

'Wow!' Harry exclaimed. 'Our boat is lying fifth and there's still a way to go.'

Henry had a tear in his eye as he watched with pride, Harry visibly willing Mike's boat on. 'Maybe you will join the crew someday soon. With all your experience you would help push them forward,' he said, patting Harry on the back.

'It is possible once I gain experience with the design team but I fear it is some way off,' said Harry as he waved his arms frantically towards the approaching boats. 'Look,' he screamed as he again focused his binoculars, 'we have moved into fourth place and closing.'

John and Henry stood back and watched, bemused. Harry jumped up and down, dropping to his knees through a combination of exhaustion and elation as 'The French Connection' finally finished in third place.

The crews one by one disembarked from their boats, climbed the harbour steps and paused a moment to acknowledge the cheering crowd before making their way over to the stewards' tent to check in. The crews from the first three boats were escorted to the presentation stand which was sited a short distance from where Harry and his family were standing. Mike spotted Harry in the crowd and marched over, his arm around a young man.

'Hello Harry, I want you to meet my son David,' Mike said proudly, 'and this must be your father and grandfather I have heard so much about.' Mike shook their hands. 'You should be so proud of Harry. He is doing so well at work; this is the first time we have finished in the first three, so Harry's magic is working.'

Harry bowed his head modestly as Henry patted him on the back. 'I've taught him all I know. It is up to you to put the finishing touches.'

David interrupted:'The presentation is about to begin.You'd better hurry or you will miss your first award,' he laughed. 'I'll stay with Harry while you collect your trophy.'

Mike smiled and winked at Harry before striding over to collect his prize.

'You're a lucky boy,' said Henry. 'Mike seems like a proper gent.You stick with him and who knows where it will lead you.'

Harry nodded his head but he wasn't really listening. In fact, everything around him seemed strangely blurred as his eyes were drawn to one of the representatives. A beautiful young lady stood out from the others, her face glowing in the bright sunlight, her long black hair fluttering in the warm sea breeze. Harry was bewitched by her beauty and when Mike collected his trophy, her face broke into a radiant smile as she placed a sash around his neck, kissing him on both cheeks.

'Who is that?' Harry spluttered. 'The girl with your father.'

'Her name is Maria Curtis,' David replied, smiling as he turned to see Harry in some sort of trance. 'Pretty girl, eh? She's English but lives in France, working for a company on the marina in Benodet on the west coast of Brittany, selling luxury boats. Talking of boats, my father has a luxury boat. Maybe we could spend a day together so we can get to know one another.'

'I would like that. I'm free at weekends, just let me know,' Harry said enthusiastically. 'You had better go; your father has been joined by his crew and is waving you over.'

They said their goodbyes and David strolled over to his father, who lifted his trophy towards Harry before he turned and disappeared back into the stewards' tent.

The following week, Harry was in the workshop at the boatyard working on a new boat when David marched in. His face creased into a warm smile as he spotted Harry.

'Could I borrow Harry for ten minutes?' he shouted over to the foreman working at his desk, who looked up and nodded his head before he continued with his drawings. David led Harry over to a table at the other end of the shop and a young apprentice brought them coffee. 'Are you free this weekend? There's a crowd of us having a beach party in one of the coves up the coast; I wondered if you would like to tag along.'

Harry pondered for a moment. 'Won't I be a little out of my depth, a boat fitter trying to hold a conversation with your wealthy, educated friends?'

David laughed out loud. 'Nonsense! They might be wealthy but there's a big question mark on the education. I know someone who isn't wealthy or posh and she would love to meet you, the lovely Maria.'

'Who? The beautiful representative? No, I doubt very much if she would look twice at me.'

'You'll never know if you don't come. Tell you what,' David

said as he stood up, 'take this VIP pass. It's for the Marina Sailing Club. We are meeting there at eight o'clock on Saturday night. I hope to see you there. I had better let you get back to work.' They shook hands and David headed for the door, acknowledging the foreman as he passed.

On Saturday, Harry arrived at the sailing club. He stood for a while in the doorway debating whether or not go in; his head was telling him to turn away. What could he possibly have in common with David's crowd? But his heart was urging him to enter; he really needed to get away from the Inn and meet people of his own age.

He took a deep breath and nervously opened the door, his heart thumping like a bag of hammers, his stomach in his mouth. Inside the foyer a doorman checked his pass before he ushered him into the private V.I.P. room. Harry's mouth dropped in awe; he had lived a sheltered life and this was the first time he had been to a club.

Music boomed out from giant speakers; he could hardly hear himself think. The room was full of beautiful people, some dancing, others gathered in groups, talking and laughing, the sound all merging together in a deafening buzz. He stood rooted to the spot just inside the doorway, his body trembling with a mixture of excitement and fear. Finally, he turned to walk away but a hand on his shoulder pulled him back and he turned to see David, a big smile on his face.

'Maybe this wasn't a good idea,' Harry said, his voice quaking with emotion.

'Please,' said David, 'just come and meet my friends; you will be surprised, they are quite friendly. Have one drink and if you still want to leave, I'll order you a taxi.'

Reluctantly, Harry nodded his head and followed David over to a group standing beside the bar. But as David did the introductions Harry looked a little disappointed as he forced a smile and glanced around in all directions.

'Don't worry,' David said, handing him a drink. 'Maria is on the dance floor; she will join us shortly.' Harry smiled and began to feel at ease as the friendly crowd chatted away. He joined in with the conversation keeping one eye on the dance floor and his face lit up as he spotted Maria heading towards them.

'At last,' David cried. 'This is Harry; he has been dying to meet you.' Harry put out his hand to greet her but she threw her arms around him and kissed him on both cheeks. She took his drink, passed it to David, and led him onto the dance floor. He couldn't believe how easy she was to talk to, so beautiful yet so down to earth and full of fun. After only a few dances he was really smitten; he felt as though they had known each other all their lives.

As they returned to the group, David winked over to Harry, 'Finish your drinks, it's time to leave.' He headed towards the door with his friends following. Maria grabbed Harry's drink and giggled before gulping it down in one, then took his hand and led him after the others.

Outside, Harry and Maria followed David's group along the jetty. Maria continued to chat away and Harry nodded and smiled, not really taking in what she was saying, just thinking how stunning she looked with the wind in her hair and a huge moon lighting up her face.

Most of the group were worse for wear and stumbled as

they attempted to board the boat but somehow managed to avoid falling in the water and were soon on deck, dancing to the music and shouting for more drinks. Maria grabbed Harry's hand and dragged him into the mêlée.

'Do you think it's a good idea to set sail with everyone in such a state?' said Harry thinking what his grandfather would say; he had always warned him of such dangers. Maria just smiled, wrapped her arms around him and continued dancing. Harry looked ever so worried as David started the motor and set off.

Finally, after some hair-raising moments, they dropped anchor in one of the sheltered coves further up the coast, where they used the lifeboat to ferry the food, drink and bodies onto the beach. Harry and Maria were on the final trip and as they stepped out of the boat the party was already under way. They were all gathered around a roaring fire, drinking and dancing.

As the night went on, Harry noticed some of the party were snorting cocaine. David invited Harry to join them; he shook his head and lifted up his bottle of beer. He had never tried drugs and had no intention of starting. Maria had been dancing and when she returned to Harry, he could see she was under the influence; she threw her arms around him.

'Just relax and enjoy yourself,' she whispered; 'try a little coke and we'll find a nice quiet spot away from the others.'

'I wouldn't take advantage while you're in that state,' Harry said, gently taking her hand. She pushed him away, snarling aggressively, before she staggered over to the main group. She grabbed one of the men, glancing over to Harry as she dragged the willing male off into the darkness. The group slowly split into pairs and disappeared into the shadows leaving Harry alone, gazing into the fire.

The following morning, Henry and John were in the workshop as they were most Sundays, putting the finishing touches to a boat they were renovating, when Harry finally showed his face.

'It must have been a good party,' said John, a big grin on his face. 'Have you just got back?'

Harry shook his head. 'They are not my type of people; it's a miracle no one drowned.' He sauntered over to the workbench to sort out his tools.

'You can't mix drink and sailing,' said Henry. 'The sea is a dangerous place to be if you're not a hundred per cent in control, that's why your father and I have always shown you the correct procedures every time we set sail.'

'Talking of sailing,' John chirped in, 'your mother and I intend to sail across to France and spend a few days around the coast. Do you fancy tagging along?'

Harry dropped his head, trying to disguise his delight. 'If I can get time off work, you could drop me off in Brittany and pick me up when you return.'

'Ah,' said Henry, 'this wouldn't have anything to do with a certain young lady from the cross-channel race presentation?'

Harry started working on the boat. 'We'll never get this finished if we stand talking all day long.'

John winked over to Henry before picking up his tools and joining Harry.

The following week John and Mary took Harry over to Brittany. He waved them off and made his way by taxi to the marina in Benodet. He slung his haversack over his shoulder and walked nonchalantly around, admiring the luxury boats while keeping one eye on the showroom. Finally, he spotted Maria coming out of the door talking to a young man. They walked over to one of the boats and spent time looking around before they shook hands and the man left.

As she made her way back to the showroom Harry sprinted over towards her and called out her name. She turned around.

'Should I know you?' she said, with a puzzled look on her face.

'I'm Harry. Remember the beach party?'

She stood for a moment and looked him up and down. He did look familiar, she thought, and suddenly the penny dropped. She shook her head before storming off.

'Please,' said Harry as he ran alongside her. 'I'm sorry, just give me five minutes to explain, then I'll leave you alone.'

'You have four minutes,' she said as she led him over to a table outside the showroom, 'and it had better be good.' She slipped inside and returned with a jug of iced water and two glasses, she pulled up a chair opposite him.

Harry was a little tongue tied; there was so much he wanted to say and he had gone over it in his mind a million times but her beautiful soft brown eyes gazing into his seemed to look through to his soul, which made him very nervous.

'I really liked you the first time I saw you at the boat race,' Harry said in a soft shaky voice. 'That was the only reason I tagged along with David and his friends to the beach party.' He paused a moment to see if there was any response but she just shrugged her shoulders. 'I've lived a sheltered life,' he continued, 'and the scary boat ride to the beach, then the drugs, was all too much for me to handle.'

Finally, she smiled and sank back in her chair. 'You must learn to relax and live life a little,' she teased. 'Where are you staying?' she said as she glanced down at his haversack.

'I'll check into a hotel. My parents dropped me off and will pick me up on their way back in a couple of days.'

'My boyfriend is out of the country for a few weeks and you are welcome to stay with me,' Maria said with a glint in her eye. 'It's okay, you will be safe; there are several bedrooms and you can lock the door if you wish!'

Harry threw his head back and laughed. 'That won't be necessary,' he said with a sigh of relief. 'I was afraid I'd had a wasted journey.'

Maria stood up. 'I'll have to get back to work. Just leave your haversack and have a look around town. I'll pick you up outside the marina gates at six o'clock,' she smiled before she headed back to the showroom.

Harry arrived back early just in case but his jaw dropped with amazement when Maria pulled up in a beautiful, white limousine.

'Don't just stand there, get in!' she said through an open window. 'I've just stolen it and the police are close behind.' Harry jumped in and slammed the door, and as they sped off and raced down the road, he kept glancing behind, shuffling nervously in his seat. 'Relax,' she said with a giggle, 'you're so easy to wind up. It belongs to my boyfriend so just sit back and enjoy the ride.'

The limousine was a surprise but what was to follow was

something else. After they travelled a couple of miles, they pulled off the main road and came to a halt outside a pair of large, ornate, steel gates. Maria pressed a button on the dashboard and the gates opened to a private road. Harry sat in silence, trying to take it all in as they travelled up a tree-lined drive, twisting and turning for a mile or so. Finally, they arrived at the front steps of a huge château.

Harry followed Maria up the steps in silence, his mouth wide open as he looked up at the huge majestic building. His eyes virtually popped out of their sockets as she opened the solid oak, hand-carved door and stepped into the hallway. The sheer opulence of the place was breath-taking, with marble floors and oak-panelled walls decked with exquisite paintings and ornaments. At the centre of the hallway was a magnificent marble staircase, sweeping up to the floors above.

She escorted him into a plush, furnished lounge. 'How big,' Harry thought, 'the function rooms of The Lugger Inn would be lost in such a place.' Maria opened the drinks cabinet took out a bottle of champagne and two glasses, and joined Harry, who had made himself comfortable on a large sofa, admiring the surroundings.

'I can see you are wondering,' Maria said as she passed him a glass. 'It belongs to my boyfriend, Mahmoud. He is a very wealthy Arab businessman. He travels the world buying and selling luxury boats. But that is enough about Mahmoud.' She leaned over and kissed him but he did not respond. 'You're so tense! Have you ever been with a girl or even kissed one?'

Harry just shook his head and turned away as he smiled awkwardly. A warm smile broke across her face as she softly touched his cheek before slipping out of the room and returning with a packet containing cocaine. She spread two small lines on the table.

'Just try a small amount; just enough to relax you.' She gazed into his eyes as she slowly took her line. Harry still looked unsure. She took his hand and squeezed it gently. 'It won't hurt, I promise; it will just help you relax and free you from your inhibitions.'

Harry chewed his lip nervously. His stomach churned and his hand trembled as he finally took his line and sank back into the sofa. Soon they were in a passionate embrace.

Maria stood up and took his hand. 'Don't worry, I'll be gentle,' she said teasingly before she led him out of the room.

Harry and Maria were asleep in bed. A gentle breeze filtered through an open window, moving the curtains to and fro; shafts of moonlight flickered across the room and the faces of the sleeping lovers. Maria lay peaceful and still but Harry was troubled as he tossed and turned from side to side, beads of sweat covering his brow. Suddenly, he cried out loud before sitting bolt upright, sweat now running down his face. Maria sat up and tried to comfort him as he buried his head in his hands. She left the room and returned with a glass of water.

'It's okay, this sometimes happens, a bad dream brought on by the cocaine.'

Harry shook his head and took a drink. 'No, it was the same nightmare I experienced while growing up. Night after night I dreamt I was one of the Barbary Pirates, plundering ships and villages, taking slaves. The frightening thing is, the same vivid faces I saw all those years ago reappeared in this dream.'

'Try and get some sleep. You'll feel better in the morning,' said Maria. Harry finished his drink before lying down; she put her arm around his and they were soon fast asleep.

Harry continued to visit Maria when Mahmoud was out of the country to engage in their drug-fuelled relationship and he joined David and his rich boat friends for beach parties with drink and drugs.

Finally, after years of studying, Harry passed his exams, and John and Mary arranged a party at the Inn to celebrate. Mike and David were there with work colleagues and of course the singing fishermen were the entertainment. Henry was playing his concertina while his two friends sang along, waving their hands to encourage the guests to join in. Soon the whole room burst into life as they raised their glasses, swaying from side to side and joined in with the chorus.

When the music finished Mike stood up and raised his hand in the air. The room subsided into silence.

'I would just like to say a few words to a very special young man who has worked so hard and is now a bona fide draughtsman and an important part of our design team.' He waved Harry over to join him and presented him with a leather briefcase and a leather-bound chest containing drawing equipment.

Harry blushed as he accepted the gifts.

'Thank you so much,' he said, his voice low and quivering, 'not just for the gifts but for your support and the opportunity to work with your design team.'

Mike shook his hand, a broad smile crossing his face. 'I have one more surprise for you, we have been working on my new boat and you have been an important part of the team. But one of the crew members has been injured and we would like you to take his place.'

Harry shook his head in disbelief as his proud parents congratulated him. Henry had tears in his eyes as he wrapped his arms around him and the guests broke out into a chorus of 'For he's a jolly good fellow'. Henry dried his eyes, picked up his concertina and once again the room exploded into song.

Two weeks before the race, Harry joined Mike and his crew taking part in the sea trials on the new boat, 'The Cornish Mermaid', in the English Channel. Training was intense and Harry was finding it difficult to keep up with the rest of the crew as Mike put them through their paces working together, robots in a well-oiled machine.

On their return to Penzance they faced a strong headwind and a sudden increase in swell. The crew automatically clipped on but Harry was unsure of the procedure. As he fumbled with his clip, the boat was thrown to one side and he was catapulted overboard. The light was beginning to fade and visibility only poor as Harry was swept in the other direction away from the boat, now in full flight.

Finally, Mike and his crew managed to turn the boat around. Frantically, they scanned the area, the worsening conditions making it impossible to locate their colleague. Luckily, Mike's experience and his ability to keep a cool head in a crisis saved the day, as he worked methodically back and forth across the area. One of the crew spotted Harry floating lifelessly and, after several passes, they managed to drag him on board. One of the crew administered first aid, clearing Harry's airways.

Harry coughed and spluttered before sitting up with a dazed

expression on his face. He had learned a hard lesson that day. Although his father and grandfather had tried so hard to drum into him that the sea was a dangerous place and that all safety procedures must be followed to the letter, this experience had certainly brought it home.

Harry was so excited as the day of the race finally arrived. All the boats had assembled in Benodet harbour and all along the waterfront a large French crowd enjoyed the festival atmosphere. Mike and his crew aboard 'The Cornish Mermaid' went through their pre-race procedure and Harry looked focused as he worked with the team carrying out their safety checks. Finally, they moved towards the start with all the boats jockeying for position and, as the starter fired a flare into the air, the race was under way. The crowd erupted, waving their flags and cheering as the competitors headed for the open sea accompanied by a small flotilla of boats loaded with well-wishers, their cheers drowned in a sea of loud klaxons reverberating around the harbour.

The fleet was tightly bunched as the boats entered the Channel; the race was in full swing, all hands on deck as they battled furiously to gain advantage. After several miles the fleet started to split up as each boat followed its planned route, searching for those slightly favourable conditions, calmer water or increased tailwind that would work to its advantage. It was much harder than Harry had imagined; his limbs ached, his lungs were on fire, snatching gasps of air as quick as he could and thinking he couldn't go on much further but determined to overcome his demons and the painful feeling of total exhaustion.

Looking around at the serious expressions on all of the

crew members' faces, he suddenly laughed to himself: he was not the only one struggling.

Mike scanned the sky ahead. 'Looks like trouble in store; try and keep focused we have overcome worse,' he said, trying to reassure them. Harry quickly looked up and quickly looked away as he caught sight of black storm clouds rolling in from both sides and a buffeting, howling wind threw the boat from side to side. The crew worked swiftly and confidently without a break amid the musky odour of sweating bodies, working with all their might to stay on course.

Tired and exhausted, Mike asked for one last effort. As they scorched along the Channel towards Plymouth, theirs was one of several boats in contention but struggling due to their boat taking in water. With Mike in control, his experience shined through as he rallied his crew, lifting their spirits to bring out a superhuman effort from every one of them.

They entered the Hooe in lead position and somehow managed to hang on till they crossed the winning line. Harry collapsed onto his knees; every ounce of energy had been exerted. But he laughed out loud as he watched Mike and the rest of the crew dancing around the deck hugging each other and the huge crowd on the waterfront cheering and waving their flags as 'The Cornish Mermaid' was brought ashore.

The sponsors had organised a celebration party that evening in the Plymouth Sailing Club bar. John, Mary and Henry were among the guests as Mike and his crew received the winners' cup. As the room erupted into deafening cheers, Mike raised his hand and waited till the noise subsided before stepping forward and raising the cup above his head.

'I would just like to thank my heroic crew for giving their all to achieve this win. Now, I'm sure you will all raise your glasses to all the competitors and of course the sponsors who have made this possible.' They had their photographs taken with the sponsors before moving over to the bar to join friends and families.

All the crew were on a high. You could feel their delight and exuberance in the atmosphere as they laughed and joked. Harry was probably the most affected by the success but his mood and his expression quickly changed when his name was called and he turned to see Maria and a man holding hands heading towards him. Maria kissed him on the cheek, took his hand and led him away from the crowd to the corner of the room.

'This is my boyfriend, Mahmoud. He has been looking forward to meeting you. I've told him all about you,' she said with a devilish smile.

Harry managed to force half a smile but his mind was racing and his stomach was turning somersaults as he shook Mahmoud's hand, waiting for any negative response. But it was soon evident that Mahmoud knew nothing of his relationship with Maria as he shook Harry's hand.

'Congratulations,' he said with a huge grin. 'Maria has told me of your involvement with the design of "The Cornish Mermaid". I am interested in building a boat to compete in next year's race but I need the right person to lead the team,' he glanced at Maria before turning again to Harry, 'and we wondered if you might consider joining us.'

Harry was taken aback. 'What? You want me to lead this team? But I'm hardly experienced enough; this was my first race.'

'I'm well aware of that,' said Mahmoud, placing a friendly hand on Harry's shoulder, 'but Maria tells me your whole life has been about sailing and boats. I'm sure Mike Williams would not have included you in his design team and his boat crew if you were not up to the task.' He again turned to Maria. 'Give Harry your phone number. I'm relying on you to use all your charms to persuade our friend to join us.' He shook Harry's hand. 'Keep in contact with Maria. I'm confident she will be able to show you the benefits of being in our team.' He smiled and patted Harry on the back before moving over to join Mike and his crew.

Maria pushed herself up close to Harry, gently fondling his face. 'I'll ring you as soon as Mahmoud is out of the country so you can visit and I'll try to do as Mahmoud asks to help make up your mind.' She kissed him, winking with a teasing smile before sauntering provocatively over to join Mahmoud.

A few days later, Harry was helping his mother and father behind the bar enjoying a drink. Henry was sitting at the end of the bar with his two fishermen friends. They were taking a break from entertaining the customers.

'Have you made your mind up yet?' Mary said, glancing over to Harry.

'Made your mind up about what?' said Henry, craning his neck. He hated to miss any goings on.

Harry shook his head. 'Mam and Dad want me to go with them to their friend's wedding at the weekend. I'll go if you do.'

'No chance,' Henry said with a shudder. 'Dressing up in neat clothes with a flower stuck in your lapel and having to be on your best behaviour? No thanks, I'll be okay here on my own.'

'Tell you what,' said Harry, turning to his dad, 'I'd rather not go and I have been neglecting grandfather, so if you lend me your boat, I'll take him out for the day.'

'Okay, if it's all right with your mother.'

Mary shook her head. 'I suppose so. You would probably only spoil it for me if I dragged you along but I can't for the life of me understand why you would rather lounge about in old clothes when you could be dressed in top hat and tails.' Henry screwed up his face and they all burst into laughter.

Harry was up at the crack of dawn on the Saturday. He was so excited, a feeling he used to experience when a young boy out sailing with his grandfather exploring the coast on adventures he missed so much. His father and mother were still in bed as he crept down stairs. He chuckled out loud to see his grandfather waiting, dressed in a pirate's outfit.

They were soon out of the cove in the inflatable dinghy heading for the harbour in Penzance and climbing on board John's boat, which was moored there. Henry opened a rucksack he was carrying and passed Harry a pirate's outfit.

'Don't laugh, I bought it from the fancy-dress shop.' While Harry slipped it on Henry took out the pirate flag he had kept all those years, tied it to the flagpole and hauled it up.

Harry's face creased into a smile. Focusing on the skull and crossbones, his mind drifted back to when he was seven years old, dressed in his pirate's outfit on board Henry's boat, with Henry wearing a pirate's hat and eye patch, and waving a cutlass in the air as Harry raised the flag. Henry would put one foot on the side of the boat, point his cutlass up the coast and declare, 'Cast off, me hearty.' Harry would respond, 'Aye aye, sir,' as he lifted the anchor and they would set sail.

Henry poked Harry in the ribs with his cutlass and Harry's mind returned to the present. Harry smiled over to Henry.

'Sorry, just the flag; it brought back memories of happy days.'

Henry nodded. 'They were that, let's go and make some more happy memories.'

The weather was fine and the sea calm as they sailed out of the harbour. In the distance the first blush of dawn tinged the distant horizon; it was indeed the perfect day, thought Harry.

As they made their way up the coast, Henry lit up his clay pipe and quietly watched as Harry buzzed about, checking and hitching the ropes, manoeuvring the rudder, totally in control of the boat and fully aware of the sea and the weather around them.

'I'm so proud of you,' said Henry, his voice tinged with emotion. 'Your progress at the boatyard and now your participation in the boat races, a true Channon with the sea in his blood. I was so disappointed when your father gave up the sea to take over the Inn, but I realised that the Lugger Inn was part of our family's history going back to the days of the smugglers when the Inn was their meeting place. I can sometimes feel the presence of our ancestors' spirits in the bar and cellar, and when I die, I too will return to the Inn.'

Harry threw back his head and roared with laughter. 'No wonder my dreams were haunted when I was young with those thoughts going through my head.'

Further up the coast there was a sudden increase in swell and the weather conditions were deteriorating rapidly; without further warning, the storm hit them. Black, forbidding clouds rolled in from all sides, casting them in a shroud of gloomy, dense air, charged with static electricity, which forked and flashed across the darkness above them. The waves were increasing in height, the heavens opened and the wind turned gale force, battering the sides of the boat and tossing them around like a toy boat in a bath, the rain lashing against their faces as they fought to stay afloat.

As the boat started to take in water, Henry struggled to his feet and staggered towards the cabin house.

'You try and keep control. I'll radio the coast guards for help.'

But before he reached the cabin a freak wave hit them, snapping the main mast like a carrot, and the rigging fell on him, knocking him unconscious. The wave knocked Harry over to the other side of the boat. He managed to grab the guardrail, stopping himself from being swept overboard.

Harry paused for a moment to gather his thoughts.

'Grandfather, can you hear me?' he screamed. There was no reply. 'Hold on, I'm coming over.'

He managed to drag himself towards Henry, stopping to hold onto anything solid as another wave washed over him. After what seemed an age, he reached Henry, who was lying motionless under the rigging. With the conditions continuing to worsen, he somehow managed to free Henry and drag him over to the cabin and down to the bunkhouse.

Harry changed Henry into dry clothes and made him comfortable before radioing the coastguard, sending out Mayday distress signals without any response. He went back on deck to try and regain control of the boat and he managed to turn it towards land but being on his own, and the boat continuing to take in water, time was running out as they limped towards shore. He could see through the driving rain a cove in the distance but the boat was listing badly, Henry was still unconscious and there was no reply from, or sight of, the rescue services. Totally exhausted and wet right through, he battled on. Finally, they entered the cove and the shelter from nearby cliffs eased the conditions but the boat was still being thrown about and was starting to break up. Harry dragged Henry back up on deck and manoeuvred him into their small life-raft before dragging it towards the side of the boat. But as he eased the raft into the water a wave crashed over the boat sweeping him overboard. He was disorientated as the waves carried him away from the boat and, as he scanned his surroundings to find his bearings and saw the boat starting to sink, he panicked for a moment. The cold wind cut through his wet clothes, chilling him to the bone as he frantically swam around but the waves helped his search, throwing him into the air, and at last he spotted the life-raft some twenty metres behind him.

Slowly swimming against the current, he somehow managed to find the strength to reach the raft and he gave out a huge roar of delight to find his grandfather inside. But his joy was short-lived as he realised they were being swept past the entrance to the cove. Again, he mustered up all his inner strength as he took the rope that was attached to the raft, tied it round his body and swam back towards the entrance to the cove. It took a superhuman effort, battling for every metre gained, stopping from time to time to check on his grandfather and take a rest.

Finally, they entered the cave and the waves pushed them towards the cliff face away from shore but Harry was totally exhausted and unable to turn the raft towards land. He had no option but to hang onto the side of the raft as they were swept towards the cliffs. He pulled his head above the raft and his heart gave a little leap as he recognised the area as a place he and his grandfather had explored in the past.

'We are saved!' he cried out to his grandfather. 'We have been here before. One of the caves was used by smugglers; it has steps and a landing area. Can you remember?' He slipped back into the water and with one final effort dragged the raft over to the cave and they disappeared inside.

It was pitch black inside and Harry talked away to his grandfather, partly to keep him informed but also reassuring himself as he blindly felt his way along the cave, praying to find the steps. He left the raft and worked his way to the back of the cave and cried out with a combination of joy and relief as he reached the first step. Pulling himself out of the water he climbed the steps onto a flat ledge clear of the water.

'It was this cave, Grandfather,' he shouted with great relief. 'We will be safe here till morning.'

As Harry's eyes adjusted to the dark, he scanned the layout of the cave. He slipped back into the water and pulled the raft over to the steps. There was a large iron ring set in the stone face that the smugglers must have used to tie up their boats.

With the raft secured he eased his grandfather up onto the steps and safely onto the ledge. Back on the raft he opened a survival chest and took out dry clothes, blankets, food, water, a flare gun, flares and a handlamp. He took off Henry's wet clothes and wrapped him up in the blankets, making sure he was comfortable before sorting himself out. Looking down on the crumpled body of his beloved grandfather, tears welled up in his eyes; the idea of losing him was unthinkable. He was still unconscious but the worrying thing was that his breathing, which had deteriorated, was now hardly audible.

Wrapping his arms around his grandfather, Harry squeezed him tightly. 'Just hang on till morning; the coast guards will start searching at first light,' he said, fighting back the tears. 'It will take more than a little storm to see an old sea dog like you off, please don't leave me.' Harry pulled a blanket over himself and used his body to keep his grandfather warm. Totally exhausted, he was soon in a deep sleep.

Harry stirred. The silence had been broken by a buzzing noise filtering through the cave. His eyes snapped open and he leapt to his feet.

'Just hang on a little longer,' he said as he gathered the flare gun and flares, jumped into the raft and headed for the cave entrance.

There was no sign of the dire weather from the night before. The sea was as calm as a millpond and across the chasm of open sky the first rays of early morning sun were peeping above the horizon, tingeing the clouds with a golden glow. As he scanned the area, Harry's heart jumped with joy as he spotted a helicopter hovering above where his boat had sunk. He quickly set off a flare and waited with bated breath.

After what seemed like an age the helicopter turned towards him. He screamed out with relief and set off another flare before dancing up and down in the boat waving his arms around like a windmill. The helicopter descended above Harry, hovering for a moment for one of the men inside to wave to him, indicating that they would return before turning and flying off.

Harry waited and waited. Every minute seemed like an hour until finally he could hear the helicopter returning. His face broke into a huge smile and he laughed nervously out loud as he watched a lifeboat following into the cove. The boat stopped a safe distance from the cliffs and lowered a small rigid inflatable craft into the water. Two men climbed on board and sped over towards Harry.

As they reached the cave entrance, Harry jumped on board and explained about his grandfather. They disappeared inside, using a searchlight on the front of the boat to light up the cave. As soon as they reached the steps the two men, carrying first aid equipment, quickly climbed up onto the ledge. Harry remained in the boat holding his breath, closing his eyes and praying for a happy outcome but dreading the unthinkable.

The two men were kneeling beside Henry, one either side. One of them tested for heartbeat and pulse before turning to the other and shaking his head.

Harry waited a while, took a deep breath, opened his eyes and whispered, 'How is he? Please tell me he is going to be okay.'

One of the men looked over and shook his head. 'So sorry, son, nothing we can do.'

'No! no!' Harry cried, jumping up and racing up the steps to his grandfather, kneeling down to feel his pulse. 'How could he be?' he sobbed. 'I checked his pulse this morning as soon as I woke.'

'Sometimes this happens,' one of the men said, putting a comforting arm around him. 'He must have loved you very much; he hung on until he knew you were safe.'

They made their way back to Penzance, the coastguards towing Harry's boat behind them. He was sitting below deck; his grandfather was laid out on one of the bunk beds. With tears streaming down his face, Harry took Henry's hand.

'I'm so sorry, Grandfather, I will never forgive myself. If only I had been able to reach the shore instead of spending the night in the cave you would still be alive.' He wiped the tears from his eyes. 'All the times you were there for me while I was growing up and the one time you needed me, I let you down. Please try and forgive me,' he whispered. 'I love you so much.' He wrapped his arms around him and broke down into floods of tears, crying uncontrollably.

A few days later Harry was lying on his bed curled up in a ball, staring at a picture on the wall of him and his grandfather on his boat, both dressed as pirates. With a knock on the door, John and Mary quietly entered the room. Mary was carrying a breakfast tray. She put it down on the bedside table.

'You must try and eat something, son, otherwise you will make yourself ill.'

Harry turned his back to them. 'I'm not hungry. I just want to be left alone,' he said, his voice hollow and empty.

Mary put her hand on his head. 'We are just worried about you. We thought you might have a fever; you have been shouting in your sleep.'

Harry just turned further away from them and groaned.

'You'll have to speak to us. Tell us how you feel, and what

about Henry's funeral?'

'I'm not going,' Harry snapped. 'Why would Grandfather want me there when it is my fault he is dead?'

John looked at Mary, shaking his head as he sat on the bed. 'It wasn't your fault, just a terrible accident. You did everything and more to save Henry. He was and still would be proud of you; no one could have done any more.'

'But that's just the point,' Harry sobbed. 'It wasn't enough. He's dead because I couldn't save him. Now please, one last time, just leave me alone.'

John put his arm around Mary and led her out of the room.

Two weeks later, Harry had never left his room. He was lying on his bed, just staring at the picture on the wall. There was a knock on the door and Mary entered accompanied by Harry's doctor, Bill Jones. Harry just lay there, his body limp and lifeless with a vacant expression on his face as the Doctor gave him a thorough examination. When he was finished, he washed his hands in the basin and glanced over towards Mary.

'Harry is fine physically but the trauma has caused him to sink into a deep depression. I will make an appointment with our psychologist, which might help Harry to come to terms with the dreadful loss.'

Just as the doctor was leaving, John burst into the room.

'Harry, I have some important news,' he said excitedly. 'Sorry, Doctor, I didn't see you.'

The doctor smiled. 'It's okay, I was just leaving.' He turned to Mary. 'You will receive the appointment in the post.' He patted Harry on the head. 'Keep your chin up, Harry, we will sort this out I promise.' He strode towards the door and out of the room.

Mary followed the doctor out and John rushed over to Harry and sat down beside him.

'I have just come from the inquest into Henry's death. The reason there was no response to your Mayday calls that night was that the air and rescue teams were fully stretched, due to the storm. The rich kids from the marina and some tourists they had picked up had taken several boats to an organised beach party. They had set off with the intention of meeting up the coast at one of their favourite coves. When the storm hit them, they were totally unprepared and each boat sent out distress signals. The rescue service responded but when they received your call there was no one at the rescue centre, so if it was anyone's fault it was those irresponsible spoilt kids.'

There was no response from Harry. 'Do you understand what I'm saying? It was not your fault.'

Harry nodded his head. 'So what? That won't bring Grandfather back, will it?' He turned over, away from John. 'I'm tired. Please just leave.'

John kissed him on the head. He pondered a moment, staring down at his son. It felt like he had lost him; there was just an empty shell left. Wiping a tear from his eye, he trudged out of the room.

There was very little change in Harry's demeanour over the following days and his parents were relieved and filled with hope when the appointment finally arrived. Harry was less than willing to go along but John would not take 'No' for an answer, saying Henry would have insisted Harry attend. The constant threats from his father did little to change his mind, but the pitiful pleading from his mother finally won the day and he reluctantly agreed to give it a try.

Harry hardly uttered a word as John drove them to the private clinic in Penzance. His mother sat in the back, trying desperately to reassure him that he would feel so much better after his consultation. When they arrived, they were ushered into a plush waiting room. Harry looked nervous; his only thought was to get it over with as quickly as possible. Had it not been for his parents sitting either side of him, he would have been off.

Finally, they were escorted to the office of Dr Jason Scott, an eminent psychologist. They were ushered into the room and he introduced himself before asking them to take a seat.

'Don't look so worried, Harry,' the Doctor said in a soft warm tone. 'This is very much an informal consultation. I just want you to relax and in your own time talk through the memories you have of your grandfather before the accident, working back in time.'

Harry glanced over to his father who smiled, giving him a reassuring nod. His mother took hold of his hand, squeezing it. He paused for a moment, deep in thought, a troubled frown on his face. He started talking, tentatively at first, of their general relationship. The frown changed into a smile as he recalled happy times, his speech now fluent, working his way back through times spent working together on the old boats, sailing days and the advice and guidance he had received from his beloved guardian and friend.

He recalled sitting in the bar of the Lugger Inn, listening to sea shanties and stories of pirates, smugglers and wreckers. Suddenly Harry became agitated, shuffling uncomfortably in his seat. The frown returned as he talked of haunted dreams and sleepless nights.

'I think we should have a break,' Dr Scott said, sensing Harry's distress and pain. 'Would you take Harry out,' he said, turning to Mary, 'to exercise his legs and maybe have a little refreshment while I have a word with John?' Mary nodded and smiled as she ushered Harry out of the room.

Dr Scott closed the door and turned to John. 'Were those dreams a problem for Harry? Would you say they were intense, regular or consistent? How would you describe them?' he said, as he sank back in his chair, twiddling his pen, his voice deep and serious.

John stroked his chin, his eyes narrowed in concentration. 'We always thought of them as nightmares. He would wake up screaming, his head dripping wet, his body hot and clammy. So, I would say they were obviously very vivid, intense and frightening, and yes, they were regular, every two or three nights when he was younger but he gradually grew out of them. We always put them down to him spending too much time with his grandfather, listening to and believing all those bloodthirsty tales.'

Dr Scott eased forward his arms on the desk, his face softening into a reassuring smile.

'Have you heard of regression? It is something, a tool if you like, we psychologists use to determine whether a problem is a direct result of an early experience or something more deep-rooted. How would you feel about me regressing Harry and maybe finding out whether those nightmares were attributed to those stories or something buried in his sub-conscious?'

Again, John looked deep in thought. 'If you think it could help; we are at our wits' end. I'll have to check with Mary but we'll try anything that might give us Harry back. He's been so distant so uninterested, we are terrified in case he does something silly.' John stood up and walked to the door. 'I'll speak with them and if they agree, I'll send him in.'

Outside, Harry was sitting on a seat in the hallway, his head in his hands. Mary was standing close by, wiping the tears from her eyes.

'What are we going to do, John?' she sobbed. 'We are losing our one and only son and there's nothing even the good doctor can do.'

John put his arm around her. 'The doctor wants to regress Harry. He seems to think it will help sort out the true cause of the problem.'

Harry looked up, anger flashing from his eyes. 'The cause?' he screamed. 'I'll save him the trouble; I'll tell him the cause. My grandfather is dead and I could have saved him but I failed him, the one time he needed me. What makes it worse is I needed him throughout my life and he never ever let me down.'

John ambled over and sat down beside him. 'I know how difficult this must be but you never let him down; guilt is a cruel part of bereavement. But I'll tell you how you will let him down, and that's if you just give in and ruin your life through this tragedy. He was so proud of you and so much wanted you to succeed. For his sake if not for ours, just give this doctor a chance. If it doesn't work, we will not push you any more.'

Harry nodded his head, stood up and wrapped his arms

around his mother. 'I'll do this for you two but then you must promise to leave me in peace to grieve in my own way and take as long as I need to get my life back on track.'

'We promise,' John said, as a huge feeling of relief washed over him. He joined Mary and they huddled together as they watched Harry slowly approach the doctor's door. He glanced back and smiled before knocking and slipping inside.

He anxiously looked towards the doctor as he crossed the room to take a seat. 'Maybe this wasn't such a good idea,' he thought, as he fiddled with his shirt collar.

'What do I do now?' he said, his voice trembling with emotion.

'Don't be afraid,' the doctor replied softly. 'There's no hurry. When you are ready, I am just going to take you back as before but this time as far as your memory goes. Don't try and force it; just say what you are feeling.'

'I'm ready,' Harry stuttered. 'The sooner we get started, the sooner it will be over.'

The Doctor led Harry over to a sofa. 'Now just lie down and relax.' He pulled a chair up beside him and produced a gold chain with a pendant on the end and started to swing it back and forth in front of Harry's eyes very slowly. 'Just let your eyes follow the pendant and try to let your mind wander free to follow its own path.'

Harry's eyes became heavy, he felt drowsy and was fighting to stay awake.

'Now, try and picture you and your grandfather out sailing,' the Doctor said in a calm soft whisper, 'and then just let your mind take over.'

Harry's eyes flickered several times before closing. He felt as if he was floating in the air, his body totally limp and relaxed.

'Yes,' he said excitedly, 'I can see we are sailing along the coast in Grandfather's boat. We are dressed as pirates and the Jolly Roger flag is flapping in the wind.'

'How old are you?'

Harry paused a moment. 'Maybe eight or nine.'

'Is that the first memory you have?'

Again he paused, then his face cracked into a huge smile. 'No, I can see myself in my mother's arms, watching my grandfather with his friends, singing in the Lugger Inn.'

'Now, just drift back and see where you end up…'

Harry's breathing became quite deep and the expression on his face was frozen as if in a coma or trance. Suddenly his face changed. A cold, strange, somewhat evil grin broke out, his eyes snapped open; they were fixed, unblinking, sending a shiver down the doctor's spine.

'Where are you now?' he whispered.

'I see myself in Algeria. It is the year 1636,' he answered in a hollow, haunting voice. 'My name is Carouy. I am one of the Barbary Pirates, sailing with a band of men led by the Flemish renegade Murad Reis.' He became excited as he went on to describe them attacking a coastal town, killing the menfolk and taking the women as slaves; he talked in vivid details of his life as a slave trader and his blood-thirsty exploits.

The doctor slowly brought Harry out of the trance before inviting his parents back into the room and sitting them down. He played back a recorded tape of the regression. John shook his head in disbelief; Mary was speechless as she gazed at the screen, wiping her eyes with her handkerchief.

Harry's face lit up. 'Don't you see? Grandfather was right when he told me my haunted dreams meant I had been a pirate in a past life.'

John looked over to the doctor for a response. He sat back in his chair and nodded his head. 'It is possible if you believe in the afterlife, or it could be in Harry's sub-conscious, planted there by his grandfather's stories.'

Mary jumped to her feet. 'It is absolutely ridiculous! I think we have made a mistake coming here. This can only make matters worse,' she said, as she grabbed Harry's arm and marched him out of the door. John followed closely behind, mouthing a 'Sorry' to the doctor on the way out.

A few weeks later, John and Mary were behind the bar in the Lugger Inn, serving drinks to a busy lunch-hour trade. In the corner Henry's two fisherman friends sat, puffing away at their clay pipes. One of them bent down beneath the table and pulled out Henry's old concertina. He played a few notes and the bar filled with loud applause. He glanced over to John, who checked with Mary for approval before signalling the fisherman to continue.

Within the blink of an eye, the bar was filled with the melodious sound of the old sea shanties. All of a sudden, the door burst open and Harry stood in the doorway, gazing towards the corner seat, and the music died. Mary rushed from behind the bar and pushed her way through to Harry. She put her arm around him and led him back over to John.

'I know, son, this must be strange,' John said, in a soft sympathetic tone, 'but life must go on. This is what Henry would have wanted; all the happiness he gave with his music shouldn't have to die with him.'

Harry nodded in agreement. 'You are right. I feel much better since the meeting with the doctor; I no longer blame myself for his death.' He hugged his parents before weaving his way over to the fishermen and asking them to play his grandfather's favourite. As soon as they started, Harry sang along and the whole bar joined in.

The following day, Harry mustered the courage to enter the workshop; it was the first time since his grandfather's death. He stood a moment, gazing down on Henry's tools all neatly laid out on the bench, tears welling up in his eyes. He wiped them away and smiled as his thoughts flashed back to those good times spent together, thoughts that had always filled him with such a warm feeling, now tinged with sadness.

John popped his head around the doorway. 'Are we finally going to finish this job?'

Harry sighed out loud. 'Have you worked on the boat since the accident?'

'No,' John replied. 'I've been into the workshop several times but I just can't seem to get started.'

They were interrupted by Mary's voice and she appeared with two glasses of beer.

'Thought you might be thirsty.' As she handed John his glass, she asked, 'Have you told Harry?'

Harry took a drink and glanced up to John. 'Told Harry what?'

John sat on the bench. 'Henry's death has made us realise life is short. We have thought long and hard about our future and have decided to sell the Inn. This will give us more time to spend on our boat while we are young enough to enjoy life.'

Harry shook his head in disbelief. 'Grandfather would have been saddened by your decision, he always said that when he died his spirit would remain at the Inn.' He pondered for a moment deep in thought. 'How about,' his face now bursting with excitement, 'I take over the running of the Inn? You could move into your little retirement bungalow, spend as much time on your boat as you wish and still be able to keep in touch with friends you have made over the years who still frequent the Inn.'

Mary turned to John, a huge grin on her face. 'That is exactly what we hoped for but it has to be your decision with no pressure from us. But what about your involvement with the boatyard?'

'Leave that with me. I'll have a word with Mike. I'm sure we can work something out as long as you are in agreement. We will talk later after I've spoken to him.' He finished his drink and gave them a hug before striding out of the room. The bright twinkle in his eyes had finally returned.

This new-found confidence faded a little as he approached Mike's office. He took a deep breath and knocked before sheepishly entering. Mike was busy working at his desk. He looked up, a big smile spread across his face as he jumped up and strode over to greet Harry.

'Take a seat. How good it is to see you. We are all looking forward to you returning to work.'

Harry slid uncomfortably into the chair, shuffling his body as he loosened his collar, struggling to find the words.

'That's what I have come to talk about,' he said in a croaky voice. 'I really appreciate everything you have done for me and I love working here and the thought of losing the Inn is the only thing that could tear me away from the yard. My parents have decided to retire and sell the Inn but that is the only thing I have left of my grandfather; all my memories are tied to the Inn. I know it sounds silly but I feel Grandfather lives on as long as the Inn stays in the Channon family. At the end of the day I feel I owe him that much…'

Mike nodded in agreement. 'I understand perfectly and in my eyes that makes you a better person. If only all young people were so thoughtful and loyal the world would be a better place.' He threw himself back in his chair and stroked his chin as he pondered for a moment or two before leaning forward, looking Harry in the eyes. 'How about you run the Inn along with a manager, finish with the boat-building team but still spend time with the design team and compete in our races? That would give you the best of both worlds. Don't decide now; give it some thought. Take a few weeks to settle into life at the Inn, then let me know your decision, but whatever that is we will remain friends, so there is no pressure.'

Harry sighed out loud. 'Thank you so much for your patience. I was dreading this meeting. After everything you have done for me, I felt I was letting you down.' They shook hands and Harry, smiling with relief, floated out of the room.

The following week John and Mary organised a leaving party for themselves and to officially hand over the Inn to Harry. The bar was filled with friends and relatives, the drinks flowing as John and Mary socialised with their guests, surrounded by the melodious sound of the two fishermen harmonising in the corner of the room. Harry was behind the bar serving drinks with the head barman, George, and his bar staff.

Harry glanced over to his parents as he pulled a pint. 'Do you think they will miss the old place?'

George had his back to the room as he filled two glasses from the optics. He shrugged his shoulders as he turned to look at them while serving a customer. 'Probably, but they deserve their retirement after so many years of working long hours with few holidays.'

Harry looked over to George. 'What about you? What are your plans for the future? You might consider becoming my manager. I will need someone I can trust to run the place as I intend to split my time between here and the boatyard. I have big ideas for this place: maybe an extension and modernisation plan. It certainly needs it but we will try and keep the quaint old Inn image the punters seem to enjoy.'

'Count me in,' George said, a huge grin on his face. 'I thought you would bring in new blood and maybe get rid of old George.'

Harry smiled as he patted him on the back. 'The Inn wouldn't be the same without you; you must have been here when it was built.'

George laughed out loud. 'Well, shortly after…'

John appeared at the bar and ordered drinks. 'What are you two up to?'

Harry shook his head. 'I'll tell you later.'

John turned from the bar to face the guests. 'Order! I just want to say a few words…' He signalled for Harry to have everyone's glasses filled and beckoned Mary over to join him. He waited till all the glasses were filled, the room in deathly silence.

'On behalf of Mary and myself, I want to thank you all for your custom and friendship over the years. It is now time to hand over the reins to Harry. The death of Henry has brought forward our retirement and although we are leaving the Inn, we will stay in touch with all of you and enjoy nights at the other side of the bar.' He raised his glass. 'Now, I would like to propose a toast to the new landlord and we hope you will support Harry as you have Mary and myself.'

The two fishermen started singing 'For he's a jolly good fellow' and the guests joined in as Harry raised his glass to acknowledge the gesture. As the singing died away, Harry put his arm around George.

'This will be a new era at the Inn. George will be the new manager we will be working together as a team, running the new and hopefully extended Lugger Inn.' Harry turned to the bar staff. 'Refill the glasses and we hope all our guests will enjoy the remainder of the evening.' He signalled over to the two fishermen and the music started up again, and the room was soon buzzing with the sound of an enthusiastic party crowd.

A few days later, Harry and the local architect Paul Robinson were standing in the middle of the empty bar with the plans of the existing building spread out on a table. Harry showed him a few sketches he had drawn of his proposals for the renovations.

'How soon can we hope to start work?' he said enthusiastically.

Paul looked up at Harry, smiled and shook his head.

'If only it was that simple. I understand your eagerness but this could be a long-drawn-out process. The Inn is a listed building and any alterations have to be approved not only by the planners but also by English Heritage. A big percentage of this type of work gets refused or at best, modified. The only work that could be undertaken without permission is non-structural work such as decoration and minor works to the washroom facilities and cellar. All I can promise is I will give this my urgent attention and submit the work drawings. I think they will accept as soon as possible but you're looking at at least four to five months.'

'Oh dear,' Harry sighed. 'Well, if that's the case, I'll just have to accept it but will you keep me informed of the progress as we go along?'

Paul nodded. 'Yes, I'll give you the good or bad news as I receive the feedback from the authorities.' They shook hands and the architect gathered the drawings and left, with Harry slumped in a chair, totally disappointed and frustrated.

George appeared behind the bar. 'Can I bottle up now Paul has left?'

'Yes, carry on, it is going to be a long job just to get planning approval, probably several months.'

George shook his head. 'Bloody red tape. No wonder the country is going to the dogs; they won't let you improve your own property without putting obstacles in your way.' George disappeared into the stockroom and carried in the crates. While Harry stocked the shelves, he paused for a moment and the dark frown on his face broke into a huge smile.

'Tell you what, I think I'll strip out the old storeroom in the cellar. At least I can do something. Will you make sure the room is cleared out by the weekend?' They finished bottling up and left the room. Harry's spirits had been lifted; once he had something on his mind he would go full steam ahead.

On Saturday morning, Harry couldn't sleep. He had lain for several hours gazing out of the window, waiting for dawn to break, but he could wait no longer. He jumped out of bed and dressed quickly before grabbing a bite to eat and a drink of milk from the fridge, then scuttled down the stairs to the cellar. He had sorted out his tools the night before. He quickly took the door off the storeroom and began to knock down the partition walls. Stone by stone, he removed a large pillar that had been built up against the back wall but as he chopped out one of the stones, he exposed a large iron ring-pull that was built into the wall.

Excited by the find, he quickly demolished the remainder of the pillar and cleared away the rubble. Things got even more interesting when further investigation revealed a straight, vertical joint in the wall at the side of the ring-pull and another joint a metre away. By this time his excitement had gone into overdrive. He slipped out of the room, returning with a grinder his grandfather had used on the boats and began to cut away the vertical at both sides to expose what looked like a stone door.

He freed the ring-pull and gave it a sharp pull with no success. He picked up his crowbar, wedged it into the joint and gave it a push but again no joy. He tried again, giving it an almighty heave, and after a few creaks and a loud grating sound, suddenly the wall moved and a doorway opened up. Harry stood there for a moment, mouth open, dumbfounded by his discovery. He felt a surge of adrenaline flood through his body. His heart was pounding with excitement and trepidation;

could this be the secret passageway in one of Grandfather's stories? Would it unlock all the questions and doubts his parents had shown over the years? His thoughts were going haywire. If only his grandfather was there with him to enjoy his find. He took a deep breath, picked up his handlamp and peered through the doorway. As he stared into the gloom of the narrow tunnel, he could hear the voice of his grandfather in his head: 'The smugglers would use secret tunnels from the caves to bring their contraband to inns and churches, to dispose of in the communities.'

He waited a few moments for his eyes to adjust before cautiously creeping through into the cold, dank and clammy air, the soft, silver light of the lamp flickering and flashing as it washed along the rough stone walls, producing weird figures and shadows that sent shivers up and down his spine. He cautiously continued along the tunnel as it twisted and turned on a slow downward gradient; his breath seemed to exhale in whispery bursts of mists and the excitement he had felt turned to stomach-churning fear. Memories of his grandfather's stories didn't help; he was imagining ghostly figures at every turn. Further down the tunnel the eerie silence was broken with a strange yet gentle sound, which echoed through the tunnel.

The walls had large brackets holding oil lamps, all the way along the tunnel at regular intervals, which the smugglers must have used to light their way. Finally, he entered a huge cavern that opened up to him. The sheer size took his breath away and the gentle sound he had heard was much louder. He realised it was the sound of the sea rising and falling as waves lapped against the rocks.

Lifting up his lamp, he scanned the area. Steps from the tunnel led down to a landing area and an old boat sat on huge timber trestles on a primitive dry dock area. Further inspection showed the boat was a Lugger. Again he heard the voice of his grandfather: 'The smugglers, carrying their contraband in their Luggers, crossed the Channel, trying to outrun the King's cutters. The smugglers would pray for fog and gales as they raced homeward and disappeared into secret caves along the coastline.'

Harry's body tingled with an overwhelming feeling of joy and satisfaction. If only his grandfather was with him to share this feeling. He continued to examine the cavern. At each side of the Lugger stood a huge tripod with lifting gear, obviously used to carry out repairs to their boats. The landing area was some two metres above sea level and the cavern was cut off from the sea by some sort of drawbridge-type wall. Above the wall a block and tackle were sited at each end and they in turn connected to a huge winch system. It may have been primitive but it was very impressive.

Harry moved back up to the tunnel entrance, turned to take another look and shook his head in awe, his thoughts going wild.

'What should I do now, Grandfather? What would you do? Maybe do nothing for the time being until I have had time to think things over.' He turned and disappeared back up the tunnel to the cellar and closed the stone door. He dragged a large wine rack over to camouflage the door, stood back and took a long, searching look before turning out the lights and slipping out of the room.

Over the following week he did a lot of soul searching. He

had to fight the strong urge to tell his parents and George. He was so excited by his discovery, he was dying to tell someone – anyone – but he decided to keep it his secret for the time being. He arranged for the local electrical wholesaler to deliver all the equipment needed to install electric power and lighting down to the cavern and he organised delivery for early Saturday morning, before the Inn opened and George arrived.

As soon as the wagon unloaded and left the car park, Harry began transporting the equipment down to the cellar, using a sack barrow and the hatch used to drop the beer barrels. He had it all safely out of sight and down to the cavern before George and the bar staff arrived.

On Sunday morning he made an early start. He rolled out the mains armoured cable from the cellar down the tunnel to the cavern, and he installed the mains isolating switch and power socket near the entrance and connected it to the cable. He returned to the cellar and coupled the armoured cable into the main power supply before going back down to the cavern, where he plugged in his portable lamp and pulled the switch, and gave out a scream of delight as it lit up.

He proceeded to fix large, fluorescent lights along the tunnel and cavern walls, finally linking the cables into the isolating switch. Standing back for a moment, he took a deep breath before throwing the lever. Again he screamed out, punched the air, and did a little jig as the whole place lit up. He decided that was enough for now; the last thing he wanted was for George to come looking for him, so he tidied up before returning to the bar.

Over the following weeks he stripped down the lifting

devices to inspect the metal cogs and all the moving parts of the equipment. Some had seized up; others had corroded with rust. He cleaned and oiled some but those that needed replacing he put in his wheelbarrow to take back up to his car and placed them in the boot.

Harry waited till George and the bar staff had arrived before driving over to the boatyard and pulling up outside the blacksmith's shop. He knew Mike would not be at work over the weekend and the blacksmith had done bits of jobs for him previously.

The blacksmith went over to Harry's car, opened the boot, peered inside and threw back his head and laughed out loud.

'Where have these come from? The boat museum?'

Harry smiled. 'Very funny… they are parts of some old lifting equipment my grandfather was working on before he died. I thought it would be nice if I could finish the job; it's something he would have wanted.'

The blacksmith inspected each piece, shaking his head and tutting as he put each piece back down.

'All I can say is I will have a go but I have to warn you it will take some time.'

'Thank you so much,' Harry said. 'There is no rush. I really appreciate the time and effort and will be forever in your debt.' He let out a huge sigh of relief. 'You don't know how important this is to me. Just give me a ring when you have finished one or two pieces at a time and I can continue working on the job.' They shook hands and Harry climbed back into his car and drove off.

Over several weeks, as soon as the blacksmith finished a

few of the parts, Harry was down to the cavern the following morning to install them.

Finally, he picked up the last parts and on his way home he could hardly contain his joy; there was an element of doubt but he was determined to keep a positive outlook and hold back any negative thoughts. He couldn't wait till morning so, as soon as George and the staff had left, he quickly locked up and carried the parts down to the cavern. He worked late into the night till everything was in place and all the moving parts had been lubricated.

'Right, Grandfather, this is the moment of truth,' he said as he walked over to the tripods. He checked the chain slings holding the Lugger before operating the pulley chain. Slowly the Lugger was lifted off the tripods and lowered into the water. Harry's face broke into a smug smile as he punched the air in triumph.

'One down, one to go,' he said. He stood back and closed his eyes. 'This is the main one, Grandfather, help if you can.' He took a deep breath as he took hold of the chain and slowly pulled down. There were a few creaks and groans, and a smell of burning filled the air. Suddenly, the sound of vibration echoed around the cavern and to Harry's amazement the wall started to move, inch by inch at first, turning into a smoother, more fluent movement.

His heart was thumping with excitement.

'We've done it, we've done it!' he screamed, as the wall continued to rise. His head was about to burst as he let out all his relief, pride and delight. The wall came to rest some seven or eight metres above the water.

Harry quickly put on his wetsuit, goggles and flippers before slipping into the water. He swam under the wall into a cave that led out to the open sea in the small cove, down from the Inn. 'How remarkable,' Harry thought. He and his grandfather had explored all the caves around the cove but had never seen any signs of the entrance to the cavern.

He returned to the cavern, lowered the wall and walked over to the tunnel to leave. He turned to have one last look and shook his head in wonder.

'You were right all along: the stories of smugglers using the Inn, the hidden tunnels and even the Inn being named after the smugglers' boats. Well, no one believed you apart from me so we'll keep this quiet, our secret, at least until we decide what to do with it.' He turned the light off and disappeared into the tunnel.

Now the cavern was sorted, Harry decided to spend time on his grandfather's boat. He felt close to him on board and got comfort from the conversation; even if it was one way, he felt his grandfather could hear him. It lifted his spirits; it was like therapy, enjoyable therapy.

One night as he set sail, the sky was clear and he gazed skyward, mesmerised by an array of stars twinkling and fading as though they were following the boat. The moon was full and the sea shimmered like silver coins dancing in the breeze. 'What a wonderful place to be,' thought Harry, 'all alone in this magical world with treasured memories.'

But suddenly, his heart sank and the warm feeling disappeared as he passed one of the coves and spotted a boat anchored off one of the beaches. Turning his boat, he sailed into the cove, pulling alongside to find no one on board. Using his binoculars, he could see a party on the beach, a dozen or so people drinking and dancing around a large fire.

'How could they, Grandfather? How could they continue these parties after the disastrous consequences of that fateful night?'

The moon shone down on his angry face. Teeth clenched, he punched his hand with his fist, kicking the side of the boat, trying to vent his wrath. Picking up a metal bar, he struck the partygoers' boat.

'They must pay for what they did,' he screamed. 'Maybe we should sink the boat and leave them stranded.' But as he set his boat up to ram theirs, he had second thoughts; a sinister smile crossed his face. 'Maybe a better idea would be to steal the boat. Well, you always told me we were pirates in a past life!' He quickly turned his boat around, glanced over to the beach and headed back to Penzance harbour.

Once his boat was secured in its moorings, he jumped into his dinghy and headed back to the Lugger Inn. He tied up to the jetty and jogged up the hill to the Inn. Inside the cavern he operated the winch, raising the wall before returning to the dinghy and sailing out of the cove and back to the partygoers' boat. Checking through his binoculars he could see the fire was still burning and there was no sign of life; the partygoers had all settled down for the night. He tied the boat to the dinghy before heading out of the cove, checking the beach again.

'Still no sign of life, Grandfather. Let us get our booty back to the cavern.'

He kept glancing back as he sailed back up the coast.

Although he was putting on a brave face, inside his heart was thumping nineteen to the dozen and he was somewhat relieved as he sailed into the cove and through the cave to the cavern, slowing down as he approached the landing area. After securing the boat he skipped up the steps and quickly operated the winch. He gave out a huge sigh of relief as the wall closed the entrance.

'That should cause those spoilt rich kids some sleepless nights!' He looked at the boat, scratching his head. 'What should we do with it now? Oh, never mind, we'll worry about that later when the dust settles.' He had one more look at the boat before turning out the lights and disappeared up the tunnel.

He had difficulty sleeping; the bizarre events of the night were going round and round in his head and the adrenaline filled him with a combination of euphoria and dread. Finally, after hours of tussling with his conscience, mentally exhausted, he fell into a deep sleep. But it wasn't peaceful as he tossed and turned, beads of sweat trickling down his brow, and his whole body twitched and shivered as he once again experienced one of his haunted dreams.

He was with a band of Barbary Pirates boarding a boat. He shouted out in his sleep, his arms swinging around wildly as he and the other pirates slaughtered the crew, throwing their bodies overboard. But instead of burning the boat as they had done in previous raids, their leader, Murad Reis, told them they would take it back with them to Algeria to sell.

Harry's eyes snapped wide open; he sat bolt upright pausing a moment to gather his thoughts, glancing over to the picture of his grandfather, a big smile on his face.

'That's it! We'll sell the boat to Mahmoud!' He looked at his watch: 6.15 a.m. He picked up the telephone and rang Maria. He apologised for calling so early but he was to compete in a race the following week and would like to meet up with her and Mahmoud. She told him Mahmoud was due back at the weekend and looked forward to catching up. Harry put the phone down, jumped out of bed and slipped into the bathroom.

Sometime later he went downstairs to the bar to join Mike and his crew to discuss details of the forthcoming race while enjoying a drink. The door spun open and two police officers sauntered in. They stood a moment before making their way over to the bar to speak to George, who was busy serving drinks. Harry shuffled uncomfortably in his chair when George pointed over towards him and the officers turned and walked over to his table.

'Could we have a word?' one of the officers said. 'An expensive boat has been stolen. We wondered if you or your staff had seen any strangers drinking at the Inn.'

Harry took a drink from his glass before clearing his throat. 'The Inn attracts tourists visiting the area, so we see many strangers but we will keep our eyes open and our ears to the ground; if we hear of anything, we will contact the station.'

'Thank you for your time.' The officers turned and headed for the door, acknowledging George as they passed by.

Mike shook his head. 'The boat belonged to a friend. His son and a group of friends were having a beach party when the boat disappeared during the night. It's a complete mystery, it can't have just vanished.'

Harry laughed nervously. 'Maybe it is the work of smugglers

or pirates and they have hidden it in one of their caves.'

Mike nodded, a smile tugging at his lips. 'You spent too much time with your grandfather, listening to his stories. Wherever it is, I'm sure the police will find it.' Mike and his crew stood up. 'We have covered all the niggling doubts I had for the race. Let's hope everything goes to plan on the day.' They all shook hands and said their goodbyes before strolling out of the bar.

After competing in the cross-channel race Harry joined Mike and the crew for the presentation and a drink in the sailing club bar but he couldn't wait to see Maria. He made his excuses before leaving and grabbing a taxi over to Benodet Marina. He stood outside brushing his jacket and straightening his tie, pondering for a moment to gather his thoughts. He glanced back over the promenade at a row of shops looking for a florist. He hurried over and disappeared inside, and emerged clutching a huge bouquet of flowers as he headed for the showroom. He took a deep breath as he pushed open the door and marched in, a huge smile on his face as he approached the reception desk and rang the bell, straining his neck to peek in to the office behind. The smile faded as a stranger emerged.

'Can I help you?' she said in broken English.

'Can I speak to Maria Curtis?' he replied as he stood on his tiptoes, looking once again towards the office. The stranger smiled and pointed towards the stairs. 'Thank you,' he said and quickly turned, rushed over to the stairs, and sprinted up to the first floor, peering in at each office around the perimeter of the building.

Finally, he spotted her through a glass door, working on a computer. He knocked and entered, and she jumped up and ran over to greet him, wrapping her arms around him and kissing him several times. She took his hand and led him over to a plush seating area in the corner, overlooking the marina.

'How good it is to see you. I was so sorry to hear of your grandfather's death. I know how fond you were of him.'

'Yes,' he replied, his face etched with sadness. 'It's taken some time but I'm gradually coming to terms with the loss. Life must go on – it's something he used to say.' He gently took her hand in his. 'That's enough about me. Have you been promoted?' he quipped, glancing around the state-of-the-art office.

She shook her head and laughed out loud. 'No, I'm working for Mahmoud. The showroom owners sub-let the office space to him; he buys all the second-hand boats from the marina to sell in his North African outlets. I am meeting him for lunch at the restaurant; he would be offended if you didn't join us.'

Harry smiled. 'That's the main reason for my visit; to speak to Mahmoud about a couple of business proposals, and of course to see you.'

'Yes, I know it's always business first with you men.' She glanced at her watch and jumped up. 'We had better make our way over to the restaurant; he hates to be kept waiting.' She put the flowers in a vase of water and they hurried out of the room.

Maria was somewhat relieved to find that Mahmoud hadn't yet arrived. A waiter escorted them to a table and returned with their drinks. Shortly after, Mahmoud appeared. Maria was facing the door; she spotted him and waved to beckon him over. As he approached, Harry stood up to shake his hand, Maria kissed him and they sat down. Mahmoud glanced around the room and shook his head.

'This is not a good table to entertain our guest.'

Harry looked over to Maria but before he could speak, Mahmoud signalled the waiter who quickly responded. Mahmoud slipped a tip into his hand and whispered in his ear, and they were quickly escorted to the best table in the restaurant, looking out of the window at the panoramic view of the harbour.

Maria smiled. 'Mahmoud always gets what he wants.'

'Not always,' Mahmoud replied, throwing a wry smile towards Harry. 'I failed to persuade you to join us, unless you have changed your mind.'

Harry took a drink from his glass. 'I have not changed my mind completely but I do have a proposition to put to you.'

Mahmoud topped up their glasses. 'Go on then, continue, I'm all ears.'

Harry moved closer. 'I would not want to move to France; I have the Inn to run and I still work part time for Mike with his design team and racing crew, but I could work for you on a part-time basis, spending a similar amount of time as I do for Mike. The knowledge I have gained working with his team could be invaluable to you but Mike must never find out about our arrangement.'

Mahmoud sank back in his chair took a drink from his glass, pondered a moment and looked Harry in the eye. 'How can I be sure you will stay loyal to me?'

Harry lent forward. 'Because of the second part of my proposition,' he whispered. 'I need you to help me dispose of an expensive boat I have acquired and there is a probability of a continued supply.'

Mahmoud glanced over to Maria. 'What do you think of the idea?'

'Why not?' she replied. 'As long as the paperwork was in order, we would be able to put them through the business.'

'Brilliant,' said Harry, with a huge sigh of relief. 'It will take me three or four weeks to refit the boat and I will deliver it to the marina with all the paperwork in order and then I can spend a few weeks with your design team.

Mahmoud raised a glass. 'I propose a toast to this new business association and hope it will be lucrative for both parties.'

Harry touched their glasses with his and took a drink. 'But I must go now as Mike and the rest of the crew will be waiting; we are due to sail back to England in a couple of hours.'

Mahmoud smiled sarcastically over to Maria. 'They came second in the race. I hope Harry will do better for us.'

Harry stood to leave. 'I'm sure this is the start of a winning team and look forward to the challenge.' He shook Mahmoud by the hand and kissed Maria before striding out of the room.

Over the following days Harry worked tirelessly in the cavern on the boat, stripping down the wheelhouse, cabin and galley, carefully dismantling each section, all the time talking to his grandfather.

'I hope you're not ashamed of me. All those times we spent renovating the old boats and this is how I use that knowledge. But you are partly to blame, telling me I was a pirate in a past life; it was inevitable that one day I would become a modern-day pirate.' He checked his watch and quickly tidied up. 'I had better go. George will be opening up soon; he will be wondering where I am.' He hurried over to the tunnel, turned and glanced back. 'Once the boat is refitted, we will sail together like old times over to France.' He switched off the lights and disappeared down the tunnel.

Mike had called a meeting at the boatyard. Harry and the design team were discussing various modifications for their boat after finishing second in the cross-channel race.

'We are getting closer,' Mike said as he sank back in his chair. 'All we need is a few minor alternations and we will be the team to beat. I want you all to put on your thinking caps; we will meet again in a couple of days to go over your ideas.'

Harry pulled out his note pad and pen. 'You get away; I'll lock up. I have a couple of ideas and if I don't put them down on paper they will have gone by the time I get home.'

Mike smiled. 'You are as keen as ever but don't work too late. We are going for a drink at the club; you should join us when you are finished.' He picked up his briefcase, nodded over to Harry and strolled out of the room, with the others following close behind.

Harry watched through the window as Mike and the team crossed the car park. They stood talking for a moment before jumping into their cars and driving off. He moved quickly over to the filing cabinet, opened a drawer and scanned through the folders; he took a registration form from one and a transfer of ownership form from another. Closing the drawer, he walked over to Mike's desk, sat down and opened the desk drawer to sort through several rubber stamps. He flicked through each form, stamping them several times; again he searched through Mike's drawer, picking out a letter with Mike's signature on. Using Mike's pen, he carefully copied the signature onto each form and as he checked each form, a huge smile of satisfaction crossed his face. He replaced Mike's letter and pen, checking everything was in place before closing the drawer and quietly slipping out of the room.

Back in the cavern, Harry put the finishing touches to the boat.

'You wouldn't believe it was the same boat, would you, Grandfather; a few alterations, a coat of paint, a new name and we are home and dry.' He chuckled out loud as he brought out the new nameplate 'Hooray Henry' and fixed it to the side of the boat. His chuckle turned into a full-blown belly-laugh. 'Sorry, Grandfather, but I couldn't resist.' He finished off, packed his tools and stood on the landing area admiring his finished work. 'A good job, don't you think? I hope you will be with me when I set sail for France in a couple of days. Pity we won't be able to fly the Jolly Roger; it might make the authorities suspicious.' He chuckled again as he made his way over to the tunnel and took one last look before putting off the lights.

That evening Harry was working behind the bar with George serving drinks. His parents were standing at the other side of the bar enjoying a night out. His father glanced over to Harry.

'Is there any news from the planning department about your application'?

Harry shook his head as he filled a pint of beer. 'Last I heard they were still waiting for the report from English Heritage.'

George chirped in. 'I told you it would take forever, too much red tape.'

'I have put it all to one side,' Harry said as he shrugged his shoulders. 'The architect is dealing with the authorities; we will just have to be patient.'

The phone rang. George answered. 'It's for you, Harry, it's a Maria Curtis.'

Mary nudged John. 'He has kept that quiet. We thought that friendship with Maria had fizzled out some time ago.'

Harry took the phone. 'It's purely business.' He turned his back on his parents as he moved away to the corner where he couldn't be overheard.

'How are you?' Maria said. 'When can we expect to see you?'

Harry glanced over his shoulder and moved further away.

'Everything is in order; I will be sailing over at the end of the week. I'll ring before I set off so you can inform the French coastguards of my impending arrival. See you soon.' He put down the phone and glanced over to George. 'Can you hold the fort for three weeks? I need to go over to France.'

George smiled. 'No problem as long as you keep in touch.'

John turned to Mary. 'We can always help out if need be. We wouldn't want to stop the course of true love, would we?'

Harry shook his head in despair and smiled at George before slipping out of the room.

Come Saturday morning, Harry was up at the crack of dawn. He had hardly slept, he was so excited. He knew the chances of being caught and the consequences but that only seemed to arouse a strong, overwhelming high, which made his whole body tingle. He grabbed the case and bag he had packed the night before and scuttled down to the cavern.

'Just like old times,' he said as he went over the final safety checks and supplies. He jumped out of the boat to operate the winch and could feel a surge of adrenaline engulf his body as the wall opened up. Back on board he took a deep breath. 'Are you ready, Grandfather? Then off we go.' He manoeuvred the boat out of the cavern into the tunnel, throwing down the anchor before lowering the small lifeboat into the water. 'I'll be back soon; I just need to lower the wall in the cavern.' He jumped into the lifeboat and sailed out of the tunnel into the cove and over to the boathouse.

The sun had yet to rise and the cold morning air sent a shiver coursing through his veins, his breath hanging in wispy, weird shapes as he raced up the hill and into the Inn. He was soon racing back down and returning to the tunnel. Once on board he strapped the lifeboat back into its cradle and they set off, sailing into the cove, heading for the open sea. He telephoned Maria to tell her he was on his way and set their course for Benodet. The sea was quite calm with just a gentle headwind and as the sun rose, shafts of golden sunlight, piercing the thin, fluffy white clouds, filtered down, bathing him in a soft, warm glow.

After an uneventful crossing he sailed through Benodet harbour into the marina. Maria was there to meet him and guided him over to one of their moorings. Harry secured the boat. Maria climbed on board, throwing her arms around him.

'So good to see you. Mahmoud will be with us shortly; he is with the harbour master informing him of your arrival.'

Harry glanced over his shoulder, feeling somewhat uncomfortable. All the self-doubts had reared their ugly heads as his mind raced through everything that could go wrong.

Maria saw his worried expression. She smiled.

'Don't worry, as long as the paperwork is in order there will be no problem.' Harry's stomach started doing somersaults as he saw Mahmoud approaching with the harbourmaster close behind.

'Permission to come abroad,' Mahmoud said with a smile.

Harry forced a smile as they climbed on board. He opened his briefcase and passed the documents over to the harbourmaster who quickly flicked over the pages.

'Everything seems in order,' he said as he shook Harry by the hand, turned and smiled at Mahmoud, stepped off the boat and disappeared through the harbour gates.

'You can relax now, Harry, that's the formalities out of the way. Now we can move to the important agenda, a drink back at the office to christen our first deal and meet up with my design team.'

Harry picked up his briefcase, gave out a huge sigh of relief and followed Mahmoud and Maria off the boat.

Mahmoud marched into the office, Maria and Harry tagging along behind.

'Close the door and take a seat,' Mahmoud said as he walked over to the mini-bar in the corner of the room. He cracked open a bottle of champagne and filled three glasses before joining them in the seating area.

'Where are the design team?' Harry said. 'I'm looking forward to meeting them.'

'They will be along shortly but first we must drink a toast to seal the deal on the boat and to welcome you to the team. I will sell the boat and keep twenty-five per cent of the money;

the other seventy-five per cent you will receive in cash.'

Harry's face lit up. He raised his glass. 'I hope this is the first of many deals.' Mahmoud and Maria touched glasses as they drank to the future.

Several weeks later, Harry steered a stolen boat into the cavern and over to the steps. he quickly tied up, jumped onto the landing to operate the winch and lowered the wall. He inspected the boat, rubbing his hands together with glee.

'What a beautiful vessel, Grandfather; this will surely bring a huge cash bonus. We will leave it for a few days to allow the dust to settle before we start stripping it down.' He made his way over to the tunnel. 'Goodnight, Grandfather,' he said as he glanced over to the boat and smiled to himself before switching off the lights.

The following day Harry was working in the bar preparing for opening time when the bell at the side door rang. George went to answer it and returned with the architect.

'I have a barrel to change; just shout if you need me,' he said and slipped out of bar.

Harry ushered the architect over to a table. 'Would you like a drink?'

'No thank you, I'm driving.' He opened his briefcase and took out a letter. 'I'm afraid I have some bad news. We have just received a letter from English Heritage. They are recommending refusal but we do have the right to appeal.'

Harry shook his head. 'No, it's too much trouble, we'll just forget about it, it would just be waste of money. They always win. If you will send your bill I will settle up and I thank you for all your hard work.'

The architect handed Harry the letter. 'Think it over; you have six weeks to lodge the appeal.'

George appeared again with two police officers. 'Sorry to interrupt but they would like a word with you.'

The architect picked up his briefcase and said, 'Just let me know your decision.' He followed George out of the room.

Harry turned to the officers. 'Sorry about that; how can I help?'

'Another expensive boat was stolen last night. We wondered if you or your staff had seen or heard anything suspicious, any strangers that have been drinking here over the past week or two – no doubt they must have been casing the area waiting for the opportune time.'

Harry pondered for a moment, stroked his chin and shook his head. 'Sorry, no one springs to mind. Do you think the thefts are the work of locals or outsiders?'

One of the officers shrugged his shoulders. 'We are not sure at this point in time but it does seem to imply a local connection, someone with knowledge of the area. The boats must be laid up somewhere nearby as immediately after the thefts the patrol boats and coastguards have been unable to find any trace.'

'I'm sorry I can't be of help but I will instruct my staff to keep their eyes open for anyone suspicious and I will inform you immediately.'

The two officers shook Harry's hand. 'We would appreciate your assistance. All the pubs and inns around the coast have been alerted. The thieves could be using them to gain the local information they need.' They smiled and left the room.

George popped his head round the bar. 'I couldn't help overhearing; these are strange times,' he smiled. 'I think old Henry was right when he talked of pirates and secret caves.'

Harry laughed out loud. 'I believed those stories when I was growing up but realised it was just fantasy and folklore.' He walked towards the door. 'We had better open up; the regulars will be dying of thirst.'

Two years later, Harry was on one of his scouting trips, searching the marina bars, looking for another victim for his lucrative operation. He was dressed in disguise: dark-rimmed glasses, a blonde wig and a sailor's hat and uniform. Over that time he had stolen a number of boats. His secret was to move to different locations for each hit, then lie low till the intensive police search calmed down before moving to his next target. On this night he followed a crowd of young partygoers into a club down on the waterfront. He pushed his way through to the bar and ordered a drink while keeping a close eye on his prey. He watched as the boys made several visits to the bar and girls rolled about giggling as they became more intoxicated.

Finally, after an hour or so, one of the boys shouted, 'Party time, drink up!' before heading for the door, with the rest of the rowdy crowd staggering behind.

Harry waited a few moments before drinking up and slowly slipping out of the bar. Outside he stood in the shadows, watching the crowd laughing and shouting as they dawdled along the jetty towards a large boat moored there. As they reached the boat, two of the girls seemed reluctant to climb on board. The boys tried to drag them forward but fell over and one of them landed in the water. All hell broke out; some of the girls were screaming, others laughing hysterically as the other boys frantically tried to fish him out. Luckily it was a clear night and the huge moon shone down, brightly illuminating the whole marina, enabling his friends to grab hold of him and pull him on board to the cheers and relief of the girls. All on board, they spent a few moments dancing about, with the half-drowned boy carried around on one of the boys' shoulders, before setting sail and heading out of the marina. Harry remained on the jetty long enough to see which way they were heading and he disappeared into the night.

Later that evening, Harry sailed up the coast in his dinghy. He stopped at the entrance to each cove to scan the area with his binoculars. Finally, he spotted the boat anchored off the beach in one of the secluded coves and through his binoculars he could see the party going on. He sailed into the cove and landed on the beach further up from the partygoers and out of sight. He quickly tied up his dinghy and crawled over to a vantage point overlooking the beach party before making himself comfortable as he waited for them to bed down.

He watched as the drink and drugs took their effect, some bodies lying crumpled in a heap, others staggering around, fighting to stay on their feet. One by one the remaining bodies succumbed to the effects. He remained there until there was no sign of life before cautiously creeping over to the motionless bodies, checking each one quietly and gently. He came across a beautiful young girl, about twenty years old with long blonde hair, and stood over her for a moment, mesmerised by her beauty. After completing his examination, he quietly returned to his dinghy and over to the boat. He quickly climbed on board, tied his dinghy up and set sail for home and the cavern.

That night he was lying fast asleep, tossing and turning as he experienced another of his haunted dreams; his increased drug use had coincided with the dreams returning most nights. He broke out in a cold sweat as he saw himself with the band of Barbary Pirates attacking one of the coastal villages. The band flooded into the village, running amok, killing the men and taking the women captive. He could see himself running into one of the dwellings, cutlass in his hand; a man and a woman were trapped in the corner. He kicked over the table in the middle of the room as he closed in on the couple. The man stood in front of the woman trying to protect her but with one swipe of his cutlass he decapitated the man. The woman dropped to her knees, screaming as she cradled his body. Harry saw himself grab her arm and turn around. He woke up and sat bolt upright, sweat pouring down his brow; the face of the woman in the dream was that of the beautiful young girl on the beach he had seen earlier that night.

He reached over to a drawer unit beside his bed and took out a packet of heroin from the batch Mahmoud had given him and he quickly took a line, trying to calm himself down and make sense of the evening.

'How can you explain that one, Grandfather?' he said. 'That can't be put down just to your stories. If I was a pirate in a previous life maybe something or someone from that life is trying to contact me or guide me.'

He lay back, deep in thought, a troubled expression on his face. Suddenly it changed into a huge sinister smile.

'Maybe that's it,' he cried, 'all the boat stealing is piracy but the next step would be the white slave trade.' He jumped out of bed. 'When I think about it, Grandfather, seeing the girl on the beach gave me a strange sensation, one I thought I had experienced before. It must have been some kind of omen.'

With the effects of the drugs kicking in he was extremely excited; everything seemed so clear. He picked up the phone and rang Maria.

'What do you want at this time of the morning?' she said sleepily. 'Could it not wait till later?'

'Sorry,' Harry replied, 'but I must speak to Mahmoud.'

'He is out of the country. He will be back at the weekend. Now I'm sorry, but I'll have to get some sleep; I have a busy day ahead.'

'Sorry again,' Harry replied,' but you both will be excited when I tell you what I have in mind; I will sail over on Saturday. I will see you then.'

He hung up and lay back down; he was too high to sleep so he just went over the evening in his mind and planned how he would put his idea to Mahmoud.

Maria and Mahmoud were enjoying a meal in their château when Harry arrived. Maria answered the door, smiled and kissed him.

'Sorry I snapped at you when you phoned but I was half asleep.' She led him into the dining room.

Mahmoud 'pulled up a chair. 'Come and join us; we started without you. I was so hungry; I always am after one of my business trips.'

Harry sat down. 'Wait till you see the latest boat; so much superior to the others. It will be ready in five or six weeks.'

Mahmoud smiled. 'Perfect timing; I intend building a new boat to enter next year's round-the-world race and should have the preliminary drawings ready for you to see by then.'

They finished their meal and Maria cleared the table. 'Take a comfortable seat beside the fire; I will bring you a brandy.'

Mahmoud moved over to a large sofa and Harry followed him. Maria returned with a tray with three glasses and a decanter of brandy; she pulled up a chair and poured out the drinks.

Mahmoud raised his glass. 'Let's drink to our continued partnership; long may it prosper.'

Harry nodded in agreement, took a drink, put down his glass and turned to Mahmoud. 'I have been thinking of ways to expand our business.' His head bowed forward, his eyes flashing with excitement, he said, 'What do you think about the white slave trade?'

There was a brief moment of silence. Mahmoud shook his head, sank back in his seat and replied, 'Dangerous business, real danger.' He glanced over to Maria.

She shook her head. 'It still goes on in certain parts of the world,' she said, her voice low and filled with emotion. 'I was involved with an Arab businessman; his name was Hamdan. He had bought a boat from the marina and we became lovers. But when I found out he was involved with a white slave operation I ended the relationship and have not seen him since.'

Harry's face lit up as he leant forward in his seat. 'I would be very interested if I had the right contacts and the rewards were high enough.'

Maria shook her head. 'You would be better off sticking to the boat business. It is much safer, we are doing very well without becoming involved with those people. Yes, there is a fortune to be made but it is so dangerous, not only from the authorities – the worst that would happen with them is jail – but the traders would eliminate anyone that might jeopardise their business.'

Mahmoud placed his hand on Harry's shoulder. 'Sleep on it; if you are still interested in the morning, I will set up a meeting with one of the top men in the organisation.'

Harry finished his drink and stood up. 'It's been a long day and I need a good night's sleep.' He gave Mahmoud a warm embrace, kissed Maria and walked out of the room.

Harry was up at the crack of dawn in the kitchen cooking breakfast, music from the radio vibrating around the room.

The door swung open and Maria was standing in the doorway, a gun in her hand. 'Is it safe to come in? I thought we had burglars.'

Harry threw back his head and laughed out loud. 'I'm too excited to sleep and before you ask, I've made up my mind to go ahead with the meeting and see what they have to say.'

Maria grimaced. 'I only hope you know what you're getting yourself into. Once in, there is only one way out and that's in a box.'

Harry just smiled as he picked up a tray and placed the cooked meals on it. 'Take it up to Mahmoud and break the news.'

The following day, Harry and Maria joined Mahmoud on board his boat in the marina. Mahmoud shook his head, his face taut and serious.

'You're sure about this?' His voice was filled with emotion.

'Hamdan has agreed to see you but he will not be messed about. Once you talk to him I will be unable to help you; he will never let you walk away from the operation. Do you understand the full implications of what I'm saying?'

Harry smiled as he clasped Mahmoud's hand. 'Yes, I do, and I know you are trying to protect me but this is something I really want – no, need – to do; this type of life is in my very soul. I will never change my mind.'

'So be it,' Mahmoud said as he prepared to set sail, 'but don't say I didn't warn you.'

Maria just looked at Harry, her eyes filled with sadness. She knew the dangers but knew Harry had made up his mind. As they sailed up the coast, the sun was low in the sky as it prepared to set and the light began to fade. Harry had a permanent smile on his face as the anticipation was building; his heart was racing with excitement tinged with a hint of danger and trepidation.

They turned into a small cove and approached a private inlet with a barrier across the entrance. Suddenly the barrier was raised and Mahmoud manoeuvred his boat through the entrance. Harry squeezed Maria's hand as he spotted two gunboats standing by with several armed men on board. One boat turned and headed up the inlet, one of the gunmen waved for Mahmoud to follow and the second boat tagged on behind them.

Harry had to pinch himself. 'Is this real?' he thought. It was like being in a dream or some high-drama action film; the buzz he got from stealing boats was nothing in comparison to this.

They followed the gunship into a large boathouse; the

men jumped onto the jetty and tied up their boat, one of the men waving to Mahmoud to pull alongside. Harry, Maria and Mahmoud climb onto the jetty. They were body-searched before being ushered into a Range Rover parked at the rear of the boathouse and quickly driven off.

They travelled in silence along a tarmac road, which ran parallel to a high stone wall. Harry's thoughts were running wild; these men would think nothing of shooting them and no one would ever know. The dangers were now sinking in but that only seemed to heighten his excitement. 'This is how the Barbary Pirates must have felt as they went on a raid,' he thought. 'This is the start of something really big – dangerous, yes, but thrilling and hopefully very rewarding.' The drugs he had taken before they'd set off seemed to have taken most of the fears away.

After a short drive, they reached a large entrance with electronic gates. The vehicle stopped and the driver typed in some sort of password, the gates opened up and they drove through. They continued their journey up through a tree-lined drive until they came to a halt in front of a huge château, much bigger than Mahmoud's. The whole front lit up with a fusion of coloured lighting. A well-dressed, distinguished-looking gentleman appeared at the front door; he paused a moment before walking down the steps to greet his guests, two armed, muscle-bound guards walking closely behind.

Maria leant over to Harry and whispered in his ear, 'That is Hamdan, the "Mr Big" of the worldwide organisation.'

Harry swallowed nervously. His legs had suddenly turned to jelly and he sat frozen to the seat as he watched Maria and

Mahmoud step out of the vehicle and approach Hamdan, who embraced Mahmoud before turning to Maria.

'How good it is to see you; it has been too long.' He threw his arms around her.

Mahmoud turned to Harry, waving him out to join them. Harry took a deep breath, sheepishly stepped out of the vehicle and walked over to them.

Maria gently pushed Hamdan away. 'This is Harry Channon from England, and Harry, this is Hamdan,' she said, somewhat relieved to escape his embrace. Hamdan strode over to welcome Harry, put his arm around his shoulders and led him up the steps and into the château.

They followed Hamdan and his armed escort through a magnificent hallway decked out with what looked like priceless paintings and gold ornate furnishings, beautiful hand-painted vases and figurines. They passed a huge, sweeping staircase covered with hand-woven Persian carpets. There were several hand-carved doors along the passageway and they finally entered a large, lavish sitting room. Hamdan led them over to a seating area, indicating to them to sit down as he reached over and pulled a cord at the side of a marble fireplace and a waiter entered the room carrying a tray full of drinks. He filled their glasses before turning to Hamdan.

'Will there be anything else, sir?'

Hamdan shook his head and the waiter left the room.

Hamdan turned to his guests. 'Sorry for the need of my bodyguards but I go nowhere without them.' He turned to Harry, looking him in the eye. 'You see, Harry, this is a very dangerous business with lots of enemies; people who will kill you just to move further up the ladder of their organisation. So you see, even I have to be on my guard every minute of every day. So you must be a hundred per cent sure if you intend to enter their world. Tell me, how do you intend to carry out these abductions and, more importantly, transport them over to France without detection?'

Harry glanced over to Mahmoud for guidance.

Mahmoud smiled. 'It's okay to tell Hamdan about our business arrangement; don't hold anything back, we have nothing to hide.'

Harry turned to Hamdan and cleared his throat. 'I have discovered a secret cavern once used by smugglers. I steal a luxury boat and hide it in the cavern. Over the following weeks I change the layout and appearance of the boat, sort out the paperwork and deliver boat and paperwork to Mahmoud.' He took a drink before continuing, 'I plan to build a secret compartment in the boat to hide my passengers during the voyage and I will deliver them to wherever you require them, then take the boat over to Mahmoud.'

A broad smile spread across Hamdan's face. 'I'm very impressed and somewhat surprised. This plan is not only well thought out but very enterprising, two birds with one stone, one abduction and one boat sold in one trip, your involvement would end once you reached France and transferred the girl to my boat. Providing she was young, blonde and beautiful you will be paid one hundred thousand pounds.'

His face changed; a stern, serious expression replaced his warm smile. His voice now had a sharp edge. 'Before we shake hands to seal our partnership, I must warn you that once you join our organisation it is for life: no get-out clauses, even for friends. No one will be allowed to put our business operation in danger. Do I make myself clear? It would be no good trying to change your mind in the future; there would be no escape.'

Harry jumped up and enthusiastically grasped Hamdan's hand. 'I have thought long and hard before meeting you and I am well aware of the dangers and consequences but I am a hundred per cent committed to the life style you offer me.'

Hamdan left the room and returned with a small case. Inside there were drugs, needles and a syringe. He handed it over to Harry.

'This is to sedate the girls so that they will remain drugged for the journey across the Channel and be safely transferred to my boat. There are instructions inside the case giving dosage, depending on length of sedation. If you will inform Mahmoud of each delivery date, we can prepare the ongoing arrangements. I look forward to a lucrative ongoing partnership.'

He shook Harry's hand to seal the deal before the bodyguards escorted them from the room and back to the Range Rover, and they drove off.

On the way back to their château Maria remained silent. She was going over and over in her head what a serious mistake they had made. Harry, on the other hand, was hyper; the adrenaline was in full flow. His thoughts were of not only the huge rewards but at last he would be living the life of a Barbary Pirate. This was probably largely down to the drugs; they were affecting his sense of reality. Maria had encouraged his drug use so that Mahmoud had control of him in order to gain the information he required from Mike's boat design but this was going much further than she could ever have imagined, taking her and Mahmoud into this dangerous world.

Mahmoud parked his car and escorted them into the château and the lounge. He poured three glasses of brandy.

'I think we all need this,' he said, handing them the drinks.

Maria took a drink and looked at Mahmoud. 'How on earth have we been sucked into Hamdan's sordid world? It will all end in tears, mark my words.' She turned to Harry. 'Please think again about what we are getting into.'

Mahmoud shook his head. 'It's too late for second thoughts; the three of us are involved as far as Hamdan is concerned and the only way out is in a box.'

Maria's face was etched with worry. 'It's not too late. I'm sure I'll be able to persuade Hamdan to release Harry from his deal providing we act quickly.'

Harry stood up and put his arm around her. 'Don't worry, everything will be fine but I have no intention of changing my mind.' He turned to Mahmoud. 'You both know the boats I supply to you are stolen and we have made a lot of money; this will be an extension of that operation.'

'I agree,' Mahmoud said with shrug of his shoulders. 'We are in now; not much we can do apart from enjoying the rewards it brings.'

Harry finished his drink and gave out a loud yawn. 'All this excitement has tired me out; I need a good night's sleep.' He embraced Mahmoud and kissed Maria before sauntering out of the room.

Back home, Harry was in the cavern. The stolen boat was sitting on the trestles on the dry dock and Harry was working below deck in the hold constructing the secret compartment. He carefully cut out a small area of flooring, putting the pieces to one side. Placing a light in the hole he measured the depth and width of the void beneath. Using his electric saw, he cut pieces of plywood and fitted them into the base of the void, up the sides and ends. He rolled out a length of flexible hose from the upper deck down to the compartment, concealing it in a storage cupboard, to act as an air pipe.

He climbed into the compartment and lay down, his head close to the pipe.

'What do you think of my idea, Grandfather? It would have been an interesting story to include in your tales, would it not?' He climbed out of the hole and rubbed his hands excitedly. 'Just the lid to make, then we are in business.' He cut a piece of plywood the size of the opening before gluing the pieces of flooring he had saved onto the plywood and fitting it into the opening. 'All those tricks of the trade you taught me are coming in useful.'

He jumped onto the hatch to test its strength, then he cleaned up before climbing back up on deck and onto the landing area. He lowered the boat back in the water, standing a few moments to admire his finished work.

'What a transformation,' he said, before he turned and walked towards the exit tunnel, a smug grin on his face. He glanced over his shoulder to take another look. 'Right, we are ready for our first passenger.' He flicked off the lights and disappeared up the tunnel.

The following evening, Harry scoured the clubs and pubs around the marina searching for his first victim. He stood near to the doorway of a club, watching the girls as they flooded through the door. Some were accompanied by men, others on girlie nights out, most of them stopping for a moment as they found their bearings and to allow their eyes to adjust. Harry listened to their accents, looking for a stranger to the area, a tourist or maybe a visiting representative from one of the boat companies. Several times his hopes were raised, and then dashed by a closer inspection to reveal they had the wrong colour hair or the wrong looks.

He glanced at his watch as he entered another club; he pushed his way to the bar, bought a drink and returned to the doorway. A group of young women danced past him singing to the music, a little unsteady on their feet. They gathered in a group beside him to sort themselves out and adjust their eyes. They were all wearing the same tops with a boat company's logo. Two girls at the front scanned the sea of bodies, then shouted over to a crowd of locals before dancing over to join them.

Harry followed them on his way to the bar and saw that they had joined a crowd from the boat set and their hangers on; he walked slowly past, scrutinising each of the girls. His eyes were drawn to a tall, slim girl with long, golden hair. As she passed by, she turned to reveal stunning looks and the most radiant smile.

'Yes,' he whispered under his breath. A huge, somewhat sinister grin broke across his face. He waited to see the whole group have a few drinks and a few dances before they staggered out of the club; he waited a while longer before slipping quietly after them.

He returned to the Lugger Inn to find several of the

regulars drinking after time. He joined George at the bar.

'Have they got no homes to go to?' he said, sarcastically.

George shook his head. 'They would stay here all night if we were serving drinks.'

Harry glanced around nervously. 'Is the front door locked? You do know it's illegal to serve after time; we could be raided.'

George smiled, nodding over to one of the regulars in the corner. 'We needn't worry; that is Jim Cole, an ex-policeman. He drinks here most nights.'

Harry washed a few glasses. He looked at the clock. 'I don't want to be too late; I'm sailing to France first thing in the morning.'

George rang the bell. 'Last orders, one more drink then home time for you all.'

Jim sauntered over to the bar and handed Harry his glass. 'Would you fill me one, please?'

Harry poured the drink. 'George tells me you are an ex-policeman.'

Jim took a drink. 'Yes, thirty years, man and boy.'

Harry smiled. 'Did you ever break the law when you were in the force?'

Jim smiled. 'I don't think having a quiet drink after time is a crime; there are lots of worse things happening. Don't worry, I'm off to an empty house, not that you would care.'

George gave Harry a hand with the glasses as one by one the regulars left.

Jim was the last to go. He looked over to Harry as he walked to the door. 'Don't worry, your secret is safe with me.'

Harry scowled in response. George waved him off.

'Don't be too hard on Jim, he is a good man, just a lonely one with no family.' He grabbed his coat. 'Goodnight and enjoy your trip; give me a ring when you decide to return.' He strode out of the room after Jim. Harry locked the door and turned out the lights before making his way down to the cellar and through to the cavern.

Sometime later, Harry set sail in his dinghy. He looked up and took a deep breath. Captivated by the dazzling night sky, the stars flickering and dancing, the huge moon mirrored on the calm rippling sea, he was mesmerised by the setting – or it could be the drugs he had taken before leaving the cavern affecting his mood, or just this first exciting operation, dangerous but exhilarating?

He passed several coves before he spotted a boat through his binoculars, anchored off one of the beaches. He slowly pulled in behind the boat, screening himself from the beach; again he looked towards the beach. Seeing no sign of life, he cautiously sailed up to edge of the beach and dragged the dinghy onto the sand. Creeping over towards the remains of the fire, he discovered bodies lying motionless around about. He quietly checked each of the girls and smiled as he found the tall, golden-headed girl.

Silently, he returned to the boat to pick up the small case Hamdan had given him. He returned to the girl, pausing a moment before taking out the syringe and injecting her. The girl's eyes flickered and she let out a sigh before her head dropped to one side. He picked her up, grabbed the case and crept back to the dinghy, gently placing the girl on a bed of blankets. He glanced back to the other bodies. Still no movement as he pushed the dinghy back into the water and they sailed away from the beach and disappeared into the darkness.

Harry manoeuvred the dinghy into the cavern and over to the steps. He quickly tied up before jumping onto the landing area to operate the winch and lower the wall. 'Just in case anyone is following,' he thought, 'no good taking any chances.' After checking that the girl was still sedated, he boarded the stolen boat to use the phone.

'Mahmoud, sorry to wake you but I'm on my way with my passenger. I'll arrive early morning.'

He slipped below and removed the lid of the compartment, placing a blanket and pillow neatly inside. Back on the dinghy, he gently lifted up the girl in his arms and carried her down to the hold. He lowered the girl carefully down onto the blanket with her head on the pillow. He adjusted the ventilation pipe near to her head before he fitted the lid back in place.

Back on deck in the wheelhouse, he opened a desk drawer and took out a folder containing the paperwork he needed. He checked each form before replacing it back in the folder and into the drawer.

'Everything checked and in place, Grandfather, we are ready to go.'

He raised the wall and steered the boat out of the cavern into the cave, dropped the anchor, slid the lifeboat into the water and pushed away.

'Only the wall to lower, then we are off,' he said as he sailed out of the cave and over to the boathouse. He tied up and sprinted up the hill into the Inn and back down to the cavern. Once the wall was lowered, he returned to the boat and lifted the lifeboat back on board. He scanned the cove with his binoculars to make sure there were no boats in view and set sail.

As he entered French waters, dawn was breaking; a blanket of mist curtained the coastline. Harry was in the wheelhouse navigating the boat, his eyes focused on the compass as he checked his bearings. The tranquillity was broken by the sound of a loud speaker and the roar of boat engines. Harry looked up to see two police patrol boats speeding across towards him out of the mist, their lights flashing.

'Cut your engine and remain on deck where we can see you,' bellowed a voice through a loud speaker. Harry quickly pulled back the throttle and his boat slowed down, bobbing around in the calm sea. 'You and any passengers stand on deck with your hands on your head,' the voice roared out as the patrol boats pulled alongside and four armed policemen jumped on board. Harry was trying so hard to stay calm. He knew any sign of guilt or alarm would arouse their suspicions so, even though his stomach was tied in knots and his legs like jelly, he managed to pull himself together.

'What is the problem?' he stuttered, his voice trembling with emotion.

Without saying a word, three of the policemen disappeared below deck while the other frisked Harry.

'Where are your papers?' he snapped, his voice cold and sharp.

Harry led him over to the wheelhouse, glancing nervously towards the open stairs. He handed over the folder and watched as the policeman scrutinised the contents. Harry shuffled uneasily as the other three policemen reappeared from below deck and strode over towards him. Harry took a deep breath. What if she has stirred or they could detect her breathing? He looked at their faces for clues but they were cold and without expression.

The policeman handed back Harry's folder. 'Everything seems to be in order,' he said, glancing over to the other officers. 'Anything below deck?' They stayed silent; just a shake of the head.

Without another word they returned to their boats and sped off, back towards shore, with Harry rooted to the spot, his emotions all over the place. He was visibly shaking; he closed his eyes and took a deep breath before returning to the wheelhouse.

'Is it worth it? I'm sure the Barbary Pirates never felt like this but I suppose it will get easier the more times you do it.' He pushed the throttle and continued on his way.

Harry was so relieved as he sailed into the marina and saw Mahmoud standing waving with two tall, well-built men beside him. He tied up the boat at its mooring as Mahmoud and his two companions jumped on board. Mahmoud embraced Harry and introduced him to Hamdan's employees. One of them remained on board keeping watch as Harry led the other man and Mahmoud below deck. Harry lifted the lid of the compartment, then he stood back as the man checked the girl's pulse. The man nodded his head, stood up and briskly moved back up on deck. Mahmoud untied the boat. Harry slipped back into the wheelhouse, started the engine and manoeuvred the boat out of the marina, and they set sail up the coast.

Harry, Mahmoud and the two men sailed under the barrier

of Hamdan's private inlet where they were interrupted by his two gunboats. Harry followed them as they sped along the inlet up to the boathouse. One of the men in Harry's boat indicated for him to enter.

Harry glanced over to Mahmoud for guidance. Mahmoud waved his hand forward and Harry cautiously steered his boat through the entrance. Glancing around he could see a motor launch moored at the other end of the boathouse and a man standing on the jetty close to the launch; he beckoned Harry to pull alongside.

As Harry's boat gently bumped up against the launch, the two men in Harry's boat emerged carrying the girl. She was quickly transferred to the launch and the man on the jetty handed Harry a briefcase and indicated they should be on their way. Harry nervously fumbled with the case as he attempted to open it.

Mahmoud stopped him and leaned over. 'Do not do that; it would be a great insult to Hamdan.'

Harry forced a smile as the man turned his boat around and sailed out of the boathouse, once again escorted by the gunboats, back to the barrier.

Back at the marina, a jubilant Harry raced up the stairs in the showroom with Mahmoud struggling to keep up. He burst into the room where Maria was seated at her desk, working on her computer. Harry strode across the room, a beaming smile on his face, folder under his arm, and Mahmoud followed close behind carrying the briefcase and closed the door.

Maria looked up. 'I take it everything went to plan?'

Harry leaned over and kissed her on both cheeks, clasped

his hands in glee and declared, 'Like a dream.' He paused for a moment and laughed out loud. 'Yes, exactly like my dream; the Barbary Pirates have been reborn.'

Maria chuckled. 'Maybe you and your grandfather were right all along.'

Mahmoud shook his head, a puzzled expression on his face. 'Have I missed something?'

Harry smiled. 'Maybe you would find it strange but since my childhood I have had haunted dreams of being a pirate.'

Mahmoud sighed out loud. 'Pirate! Most children all over the world will probably have had that same dream.'

Harry's face changed; his tone became serious. 'Yes, but how many of those children in later life have been regressed by a psychologist and experienced those same vivid images in a past life under hypnosis?'

Mahmoud's eyes narrowed; he frowned in disbelief. He stood silent for moment.

'Maybe that is true and I suppose if you believe in the afterlife it would be inevitable that you should relive that past life.'

Maria interrupted. 'Let us return to the business side of things. Regardless of what we all think, we are living in the here and now. We should not get carried away; one success does not make it safe. The next hit will be more tricky as the authorities will be prepared; one mistake on our part and it's curtains for us all. If the police don't catch us then Hamdan will eliminate any sign of discovery.' She took out a file from her desk drawer. 'Right, now you have delivered the boat, I need the paperwork.'

Harry placed the folder on the desk and took out the forms,

handing them to Maria.

'I think you will find everything in order and you're right, we can do this as long as we are not too greedy and plan everything meticulously before acting.'

'Good. We must keep our feet firmly on the ground, and I now believe we can succeed. Right, you will receive your share of the money once Mahmoud has sold the boat on.'

Mahmoud stepped forward, opened the briefcase and turned it upside down, and the bundles of notes cascaded onto the desk.

'We have dealt with the main course; now for dessert, the icing on the cake.' He counted the money out – $100,000. He gave Harry $75,000 and Maria the other $25,000. 'Not bad for a day's work.'

Maria sauntered over to the drinks cabinet and returned with three glasses and a bottle of champagne.

'I think a toast is in order.'

Mahmoud cracked open the bottle and filled the glasses. 'To the first of many such big fat paydays,' he said as he threw back his head and laughed out loud. 'Maybe we were all Barbary Pirates in that life, Harry.' Harry shook his head, a little upset. 'It's only a joke; part of me does believe you. Anyway, are you staying a few days to work with my design team? The preliminary drawings for the new boat are complete.'

'Yes, of course, I'm looking forward to seeing them and I plan to stay for a couple of weeks to spend some of my ill-gotten gains.'

The three of them drank to that.

'Come, I will treat you to a slap-up meal at the finest

restaurant in Benodet.'

Maria jumped up and danced towards the door. 'Anyway, I would rather live like kings than Barbary Pirates,' she giggled, as she slipped out of the room with Harry in hot pursuit. Mahmoud just chuckled to himself as he sauntered after them.

Two years later, the Benodet sailing club was hosting the presentation awards for the round-the-world boat race. The club was packed to the rafters with sponsors, competitors, their families and friends. The final trophy, the winners' cup, sat on display on the stage area, which was draped with banners and flags advertising the sponsors. A representative from the main sponsors stood behind the cup, flanked on either side by several girls wearing their colours and logos.

One of the girls was Maria; she was representing the marina showroom and stood alongside the cup. Mahmoud marched up the steps onto the stage, cheered on by an ecstatic crowd. He was congratulated by the main sponsor and handed the cup. Maria stepped forward and placed her sponsors' sash around him, kissing him on both cheeks to the eruption of cheers around the room. In the crowd standing at the bar, Mike his son David, Harry and their boat crew were drinking from the cup they had won for finishing in second place.

Mike shook his head and glanced over to Harry. 'I don't know how Mahmoud keeps on winning, he must have a strong design team; he always seems to be one jump ahead of us.'

David nudged Harry in the ribs as he nodded over to Maria with a mischievous grin. 'Have you seen Maria? You were keen on her at one time.'

Harry just laughed. 'She chose Mahmoud. Just maybe the

château and millionaire's life style might have had something to do with it.' Mike and the crew joined in with the laughter.

Mahmoud led Maria and the girls down the steps towards the bar, pushing through a sea of cheering fans. Mahmoud ordered champagne, glanced over to Mike and beckoned him over to join them. Mike declined but put up his hand to acknowledge Mahmoud's victory.

Maria weaved her way over, kissed Mike and his company, grabbed his hand and dragged him over to join Mahmoud and the girls. Mike shook Mahmoud's hand. Maria pulled David forward.

'This is Mike's son, David, and you remember Harry; we met him at the presentation in England a few years ago.' She winked at Harry as Mahmoud shook Harry's hand.

Mahmoud ordered more champagne and topped up everyone's glasses, just as a crowd of the young, local rich kids danced past, grabbing hold of the girls standing with Mahmoud.

'We are off to a beach party and you girls are all invited.'

The girls looked at Mahmoud and shrugged their shoulders as they tagged onto the dancing train of bodies heading for the exit.

Harry turned to David. 'It's just like home, girls attracted to money and boats.'

David smiled and nodded in agreement.

Mike finished his drink. 'Thank you, Mahmoud; we must be leaving as we have an early start back to England at first light. I hope we can give you a closer race next year; we are working on something quite exciting.'

They all said their goodbyes before leaving. Harry was the

last to drink up. He smiled at Mahmoud and mouthed, 'See you soon,' before following Mike and his crew out of the room.

A few months later, Harry was in the cavern. He had just finished working on his latest stolen boat and he stood back to admire his work.

'What do you think, Grandfather? Another perfect refit. I'm getting better and faster the more I do. Just the compartment to sort out then we are off to France.'

The drugs had finally killed the sensitive, shy, honest boy he had once been; he had lost touch with reality and with what was right and wrong. The act of deceiving Mike, who had been like a second father to him, was bad enough but the abduction of young innocent girls without a thought to their families or what kind of life they would have is hard to comprehend. He really had the mindset of those Barbary Pirates in his nightmares now.

He carried his tools below deck and marked out the opening on the floor, stroking his chin as he paused for a moment. He stood up and looked down on the marked area.

'This boat must be larger than the others; the floor area is much wider. Maybe we could carry two passengers; that would really be worthwhile.'

He carefully cut out a small section of flooring, putting it to one side. He lowered his handlamp into the void. He lay flat on the floor, popped his head over the side and cried out with glee, 'Yes, yes, there is room for two girls.' He gave out a blood-chilling cackle. 'They will be able to keep each other company.'

He proceeded to mark out the larger opening. When he had cut it out, he lined it with plywood. Once he had completed the lid, he laid out a bed of blankets and positioned the air pipe before placing the lid over it. He cleared up the mess, packed up his tools and stepped out onto the landing area. He rubbed his hands.

'Now let us go and look for two passengers.' Again, he let out a cold, high-pitched shriek, which echoed around the cavern. He strode over to the exit, switched off the lights and disappeared into the tunnel.

The following week, Maria was in her office. She pulled open the filing cabinet, flicking through files. As the door swung open, she turned to see Mahmoud struggling with his luggage. He slammed the door shut with his foot, dropping his cases before striding over to Maria to wrap his arms around her in a warm embrace.

'I've missed you so much. I'm sorry for my delayed arrival; my business negotiations in Algeria took longer than expected.' She poured him a coffee. He took a drink as he sauntered over to her desk, picked up the mail and flicked through. 'Have you spoken to Harry?' he said, without raising his head.

'Yes, I told him you were delayed. He understood and was going ahead with delivery to Hamdan on his own today. He should be joining us shortly.'

She opened her laptop and began to type; Mahmoud continued to skip through his mail. The telephone rang and Maria picked it up. She glanced over to Mahmoud and put her hand over the phone.

'Do you want to speak to your man in Algeria – Hassan?'

He nodded as he sauntered over to her desk and took the phone, while Maria carried on typing.

The office door swung open and Harry waltzed in, carrying two large briefcases. He closed the door and stood with a huge smile, beaming from ear to ear, as he struggled to control his jubilation. Mahmoud indicated he would only be a couple of minutes.

Harry swept past to embrace Maria.

'Were there any problems?' she asked. Harry shook his head, ambled over to the centre of the room and emptied the two cases on the floor. Mahmoud looked up, his eyebrows raised, and quickly finished the call to join Harry on the floor.

Harry grabbed a fistful of notes, threw them up in the air and laughed out loud, hysterically. 'I have a little surprise bonus. I transported two passengers over to Hamdan; two girls twice the price.'

Mahmoud looked amazed. 'How? Why?'

Harry jumped to his feet. 'I need a drink and a sit down, and then I will explain.'

Maria took a bottle of champagne and three glasses over to the seating area and they sat down in silence, having a drink to gather their thoughts.

Maria shook her head, her face creased with anxiety. 'You're becoming too greedy. Where will you go to next? This is a recipe for disaster. You will get caught if you don't get a hold of this.'

Harry took a drink. 'You worry too much; it is the same risk one, two or more girls. Same risk, greater reward.'

Maria's eyes flashed with anger and fury. 'This is not your decision. We are all in this together. You get caught and we will all end up in jail. What you are forgetting is that, up till now, each girl that has gone missing, the authorities have put down to them maybe taking a midnight swim under the influence of drink or drugs and then drowning, but now it's two girls from the same party they will delve deeper; it will not take them long to come up with the answer.'

Mahmoud, who had remained silent, took a deep breath as he sank back in his chair. 'It's too late to talk of this one but Maria's right; you can't take decisions like that without talking to us – and what about Hamdan? Is he okay with this new arrangement?'

'Yes, he was more than okay. He said the more the merrier for all parties. That made me think we could supply even more girls.'

Maria put her hands in the air in despair. 'No way! The more girls go missing, the greater the pressure on the authorities to solve the case.'

'Please just listen to what I have to say. It was you, Maria, that gave me the idea when you were in the sailing club with the crowd of female representatives. How easy it would have been for Maria to slip a tablet into two of the girls' drinks and I could have followed them out and led them down to the beach.'

Mahmoud chirped in. 'It sounds easy but how would you get the girls off the beach?'

Harry leant forward, an excited look in his eyes. 'I believe I have hatched a fool-proof plan. The boat I just delivered has a compartment large enough for two girls so we would use the same boat to abduct two girls from England, deliver them to Hamdan, then take two from Benodet's beach and back to Hamdan; one operation, four girls.'

Maria shook her head. 'It's just too risky, too near home.

The thing that frightens me most is you are not doing this for the money; it is to feed your obsession with wanting to be the Barbary Pirate that you were in that past life. Please just be satisfied with the way things have been going. It's much safer, and if you think about it you are already living the life of a Barbary Pirate, really evil. These girls are someone's daughters. Is that not enough?'

Harry rubbed his chin and paused for a moment. 'Tell you what – just give it a try, a dummy run. We will go through the motions and if at any time you are unhappy, we will not go through with the abductions.'

Mahmoud nodded. 'Sounds good to me but we will leave that final decision as to whether or not we go through with the final part of the operation to Maria.'

'Okay,' she said, 'but it's with a huge question mark; it sounds so easy but we will see on the night what problems arise.'

They drank a toast to the idea before dividing out the money.

Back in Cornwall there was a huge outcry and media coverage of the two girls that had gone missing. The whole area was swarming with police and reporters from around the world. Just as Maria had predicted, the authorities now believed the girls had been abducted and were using all their resources to solve the case, so they closed down. Harry would have no more trips to the bars or over to France. Mahmoud had told him no more boats until the dust had well and truly settled.

Over the following months the reporters slowly dwindled away and the authorities, unable to find any leads, pulled back. The case remained open but they had exhausted all possible avenues and Harry was very relieved to see it fizzle out. It had made him wonder and, of course, worry. But the urge inside him to carry on was so overwhelmingly strong, he started once again to roam the bars and clubs further up the coast.

Finally, after some six months, he found a boat and a beach party in an isolated bay. It was too much of a temptation and he headed back to the Inn to lift the wall, the adrenaline once again pulsating through his veins. As he sailed back with the stolen boat, the drugs had numbed the fear and he once again felt alive. Nevertheless, if he was honest, there was a feeling of great relief as he entered the cavern and lowered the wall. The following day he rang Mahmoud to give him the news and tell him that he would be in touch once the boat had been refitted, but he would not rush things and would wait till the investigation that would follow the theft had taken its course.

Harry worked on the boat over the following weeks and watched as the media and police presence around the area faded and fizzled out before once again starting his night-time search of the clubs and bars. At long last, Maria informed him of a pending boat show in Benodet and agreed to go ahead with his plan, even though she was not fully behind it; she stressed that at the slightest hint of things not going to plan he must abort the abduction.

Harry worked very hard over the following weeks to finish the refit in time for the boat show in Benodet. Once completed he set his mind on finding a victim. One night, after another fruitless evening, he watched the last of the bars close, so frustrated after Maria had finally agreed to give his plan a go. Back on board his dinghy, he decided to go for a sail around the coast; the drugs he had taken earlier had kicked in and his mind was all over the place. It would be no good going back to the Inn as he would never be able to sleep, so he sailed on and on, much further than his usual trips. Just as he decided to turn back, he saw a glow coming from one of the small, isolated bays further up.

He continued forwards and slowed down at the entrance. He took out his binoculars and could see a boat in the bay and a party on the beach. He entered the bay, staying in the shadows of the cliffs, slowly moving towards the beach with his engine turned off. Through his binoculars he could see the party going on so he pulled in to the side and waited. He kept checking and gradually the partygoers bedded down for the night. He waited till the last ones settled down and gave them half an hour to make sure before quietly moving forward with his engine switched off. He paddled to the beach away from the party.

He stood for a moment, deep in thought. Should he take a closer look? Maybe there were no suitable girls there; with all the other abductions, he had known his victims, having followed them from the marina. He decided it was too much of a risk.

He turned to go back; it was too much of a gamble. He could be discovered, and all for nothing. He climbed back into his boat but as he sailed away, his obsession took over. That was part of his addiction; the danger, the chance of being caught gave him such a buzz. So he turned back and took the boat up to the beach, just out of sight of the party but near enough to carry his victims back if he found them.

He took out his briefcase with the drugs and crept over to the sleeping bodies. One by one he knelt over each girl to take a closer look. He found one; she was blonde and pretty. Maybe he should just be satisfied with her. But again, his compulsion spurred him on; he left her and continued his search. Just as he was about to settle for only one, his heart leapt with joy and he struggled to stop himself shouting out as he came across a real beauty – a gorgeous blonde with angelic looks.

He glanced around to make sure no one was stirring before administering the drug to her. He gently picked her up and tiptoed back to the other girl. After drugging her, he carried the first girl back to his boat, laid her inside and covered her up before returning and picking up the other girl. With both girls comfortable, he set sail for home.

Back at the cavern he transferred the girls into the stolen boat and checked his watch.

'It's a bit early don't you think, Grandfather? If we leave now, we'll reach Hamdan's by dawn. But I doubt whether he'll mind and it will give us plenty of time to prepare for Maria's party.'

He raised the wall and, once he had been back to the cavern and lowered the wall, set sail without further ado.

The weather was good and calm, and a tail wind pushed him on. He was soon sailing up the inlet with Hamdan's gunboats. He handed over his cargo before returning to the marina in Benodet.

That night, Harry stood close to the doorway of the club holding a drink as he watched Maria and a crowd of female representatives celebrating after the boat show. He smiled to himself as he saw Maria organising a drinking competition between the girls. They laughed, giggled and cheered as they encouraged each other to down each drink. Maria discreetly poured the drinks into the glasses of the other girls as she joined in with the cheers. She suggested they move to another club after one more drink and, pushing her way to the bar, ordered the drinks.

Harry casually sauntered over beside her but did not acknowledge her. She arranged the drinks on a tray, placing two of them to one side, and turned her back for a moment to allow Harry to slip a tablet into the two drinks.

Maria danced her way back to the girls, passing the drinks around, making sure the two blonde beauties received the spiked drinks. She finished her own drink and, once the girls had all finished theirs, she led them doing the Congo as they weaved their way through the crowd, passing Harry on their way out. Harry gave them a few minutes, finished his drink and followed them out.

Outside he could see Maria leading the Congo chain down onto the beach. Harry rang Mahmoud to tell him to bring the boat into the harbour and followed the girls, keeping well out of sight in the shadows. Maria waited till the two victims were struggling to stay on their feet.

She broke up the chain and ran off shouting, 'Last one to the bar pays for the drinks,' as she headed back to the promenade, with the girls struggling to keep up.

Harry, keeping to the shadows, moved forward. He saw the two girls stagger for a few metres before they collapsed, one on top of the other. He rushed towards them, telephone in his hand.

'Mahmoud, bring the lifeboat to the beach; all systems go.'

He waited till he saw the lifeboat heading towards them before gently carrying the girls to the shoreline and he waved Mahmoud to come in. Mahmoud threw Harry a rope and he pulled the boat ashore. Mahmoud passed his briefcase to Harry, who administered the injections before placing the two girls into the boat. He pushed the boat off the beach and jumped on board as Mahmoud steered them out towards the anchored boat in the harbour.

The following evening, back at the Lugger Inn, George was behind the bar serving drinks. Jim Cole, the ex-policeman, was propped up against the bar watching the TV in the corner of the room.

'Is Harry about?' he asked George.

'No,' he replied, 'he's in France again on one of his trips. It's all right for some,' he laughed as he pulled a pint.

Jim shook his head. 'What's the attraction? He seems to spend more time over there these days.'

George shrugged his shoulders and smiled. 'I think he's in love. He spends his time with a young woman he met over here but she lives in France.' He filled a tray with pints of beer and carried them over to a group of regulars sitting in the corner, playing dominoes. He had a few words with them before returning to the bar and filling Jim's glass. George glanced over to the regulars.

'They tell me two girls have gone missing.'

Jim shook his head. 'Yes, I heard. What with the stolen boats and missing girls the area is going back to the days of pirates and smugglers.' He glanced over to the TV. 'Turn the sound up.'

There was silence for a few moments. 'Did you hear that? Now two girls have gone missing on the west coast of France around the marina in Benodet.'

George shook his head. 'I don't believe it; that's where Harry's girlfriend works.'

Jim stroked his chin as he pondered for a moment. 'Yes. I wonder whether there is any connection to the two over here in Penzance. Maybe the same gang, seems too much of a coincidence.' He finished his drink. 'I'm off for my lunch.' He strode out of bar and waved at the regulars as he passed by.

The following year, Maria and a group of female reps from Benodet marina were attending a two-day boat show in Penzance; the sponsors were paying for a well-earned drink in one of Penzance's favourite clubs. Harry and Mahmoud were there to support the show and were standing at the bar.

Maria pushed her way through the crowd to order the drinks for the girls. Harry stepped to one side to allow her in. She handed the barman a list of drinks and turned to Harry and Mahmoud.

'Would you like a drink?'

Harry smiled and shook his head. 'I'm keeping sober just in case one or two girls would like a lift.'

Mahmoud burst into fits of laughter.

Maria turned, her eyes flashing. 'Don't even think about it. These girls are my friends.' She picked up the tray of drinks and scowled at Harry before weaving her way back through the crowd to join the girls.

Mahmoud laughed. 'You've really upset her; best keep out of her way for a while. Oh, by the way, how is the latest boat coming along?'

'Everything is in order; I've just sorted the paperwork out this morning.'

'Very good, but best leave it a couple of days till Maria and I have returned to France. No good taking unnecessary risks.'

Harry nodded, a wry smile on his face. His eyes had locked onto two young blonde girls who had just walked into the club on their own. He watched as they stood at the doorway for a moment or two before making their way to the bar a little further along from where Harry was standing.

He passed Mahmoud his drink before casually sauntering over, near to them, and looked around as though looking for someone. One of the girls beckoned the barman over and ordered their drinks speaking in a broad Australian accent. The other girl asked for ice and she too was Australian.

Harry's face lit up as he returned to Mahmoud who shook his head.

'O-Oh, I've seen that look before. Maria will go off on one if we ignore her wishes.'

Harry smiled. 'I know, but it's too good an opportunity; the girls are on their own and from Australia. I doubt if anyone will miss them for weeks.'

Mahmoud nodded. 'I agree, it does seem a shame to allow a golden opportunity to pass by.'

'Good,' Harry said. 'I'll bring the dinghy back to the marina and wait for your phone call before coming ashore.'

Mahmoud put his hand in his pocket. 'Yes, I have a packet of tablets so I can spike their drinks.'

'Right,' Harry said as he finished his drink. 'Don't take any risks; if I don't receive your call, I'll simply return home. Say goodbye to Maria,' he said before he slipped out of the room.

Harry sailed into the harbour, lowered the lifeboat into the water and waited patiently for Mahmoud to call. Just as he was about to give up hope, the phone rang and Mahmoud said he was waiting for the tablets to take effect. Harry climbed into the lifeboat and sailed towards the shoreline, coming to a halt a few hundred metres away. Finally, he received the call and headed towards the shore. He could see Mahmoud waving his arms. They soon had the two girls on board and set off back to the cavern.

The following day, Jim Cole strode into the police station in Penzance, his face taut with pain as he rushed up to the desk sergeant.

'Could you tell my old colleague, DI Paul Homes, I need to discuss some urgent business.'

'Take a seat while I check he is free to see you,' said the sergeant as he disappeared along the corridor.

He returned minutes later and beckoned Jim to follow him. Jim knocked on the door before he entered the room. Paul strode over to shake his hand.

'It's so good to see you. Take a seat and tell me how I can help you.'

Jim sat down and put his head in his hands.

'My daughter and her friend have gone missing.'

Paul pulled his chair closer.

'I thought she was in Australia with your ex-wife.'

'She was,' Jim said, fighting back his tears. 'This was her first trip over here since they moved there fifteen years ago.' Again he slumped forward, head in hands. 'The first time she visits and she goes missing. God only knows what her mother will say.'

Paul took out a bottle of brandy from his drawer and filled two glasses.

'Are you sure she's gone missing?' he said as he handed Jim a glass. 'Maybe she tagged along with the boat crowd and ended up at an all-night beach party.'

'I doubt that. I warned her of the dangers and the spate of missing girls in the area.'

'Just give it a few hours to see if she returns; if not I'll instigate a full-scale search.'

Jim finished his drink. 'Thanks for listening. I'll stay in touch but I have such a bad feeling about this; if she has been abducted, every minute counts. Please don't leave it too long.' They shook hands and Jim marched out of the office.

Finally, after what seemed like days, Paul rang to inform him he had started the search. Jim grabbed a few photographs of his daughter before he hurried out of his house and over to the marina. He scoured the pubs and clubs with the photos to question the doormen and the marina revellers and he stayed there till the last bar had closed and the whole place was deserted before returning home. He found it impossible to sleep and left the television on but his eyes were heavy. Just as he started to nod off, the telephone rang. He sat bolt upright, his eyes now wide open as he jumped up and grabbed the phone.

'Jackie is that you?' he screamed.

His face fell; Paul was on the other end of the line.

'Sorry to startle you but I promised to keep you up to date. Your daughter and her friend were seen in two of the clubs that night. One of the doormen saw them leave the sailing club in a drunken state, staggering towards the beach. We have the coastguards and police divers searching the waters in the marina as we speak. Are you still there, Jim?' He repeated himself several times before Jim responded.

'Yes, sorry, I just need time to get my head around that news, and I'll appreciate it if you don't disclose to the media that the girl is my daughter.'

He put the telephone down and sank back into his chair. He stared vacantly in front of him at the television as it showed the news headlines: 'Two girls go missing on the west coast of Franc.' He shook his head, brought back to his senses with a jolt. He sat up as the news continued, showing the marina in Benodet. Jim put his head in his hands, deep in thought. He had a flashback of George in the Lugger Inn ringing in his head.

'Harry's girlfriend works in the marina in Benodet.'

He jumped to his feet, crying out 'gotcha' as he straightened his tie, slipped on his coat and strode out of the room.

The bar door swung open. Jim rushed in; he stood for a moment to calm down, took off his coat and, although his heart was pounding with anger and frustration, he managed to saunter casually over to the bar.

George looked up. 'Usual, Jim?'

Jim nodded his head. 'Is Harry about?' he asked, his voice shaking with emotion.

'No, he's over in France again. It's all right for some,' George replied as he filled Jim's glass and put it on the bar top.

Jim took a drink, his face flushed as he loosened his tie, closed his eyes and took a deep breath, struggling to stay in control.

'France — I was just speaking to him the other day; he didn't mention this trip.'

George smiled. 'He never tells me until the last minute; it always seems to be a spur-of-the-moment thing with him.'

'Is it always Benodet or does he tour about?'

'No, it's always Benodet and he usually stays in his girlfriend's château for two or three weeks, lucky devil.'

Jim forced a smile and drank up. 'Well, I'll be off. I'm meeting an old friend of mine for a drink in Penzance.' He grabbed his coat before he slipped out of the bar.

Sometime later, Jim entered the bar in the police social club. He spotted Paul and a bunch of colleagues standing at the bar, laughing and joking as they enjoyed a drink after work.

Jim weaved his way through the crowded room. Several of the officers shouted jibes as Jim passed by. Paul turned to see what the commotion was about. He spotted Jim and beckoned him over to join them.

Jim again tried to act naturally as he struggled to hide his grief.

'Could I have a word in private?'

One of the officers cried out, 'He's after his old job back; don't listen, we had enough of him,' he taunted.

Jim forced a grin. Paul put his arm around him as he led him over to a quiet table in the corner of the room.

'Sorry about the lads but they don't know about your daughter.'

Jim nodded. 'I know. I appreciate your discretion. Have you heard about the missing girls in France?'

Paul nodded. 'Yes, I saw the news.'

Jim checked there was no one within earshot. 'Is there any connection with the Penzance case?'

'Sorry, you know that's confidential information.'

Jim paused. 'Yes, okay, but can you check something for me? I think Harry Channon from the Lugger Inn is involved somehow; he has a girlfriend in Benodet in France and goes there at regular intervals. She works in the marina over there and Harry was there last night, so please give me a lead, I beg you, so I can try and save my daughter if it's not already too late.'

Paul rubbed his chin and paused for a moment before looking Jim in the eyes.

'What I'm about to tell you must not be repeated, otherwise I'll be joining you in retirement. Interpol are involved and that is top secret. I can tell you we think there is some connection between the stolen boats and the missing girls. Once a boat is stolen there is several weeks lapse before the girls go missing. It's always the same pattern.'

Jim sighed with relief. 'Thank you so much. I swear I will not repeat anything you have told me and if Harry is involved, I intend to find proof.'

'Very good. If you do come up with any evidence give me a call, day or night, and I will investigate.'

Jim stood up. 'Thanks again; you have given me hope and I will keep you informed of any progress.' They shook hands before Jim pushed his way back through the crowd on his way out, and once again several of the officers shouted and goaded him.

Jim was so convinced Harry was involved, he put his life on hold to concentrate on finding the proof needed to warrant

Paul to investigate. So, night after night, dressed in disguise, he followed Harry around the marina and the clubs. It turned into an obsession and he found it difficult to sleep as the nights slipped by. He knew time was not on his side and his daughter's life depended on him; once she was taken out of the country, the trail would go cold and she would be lost forever.

One night, he followed Harry through the marina into one of the clubs. He watched as Harry ordered a drink at the bar and scanned the groups of revellers around him. He waited till a group of rich kids, boys and girls, finished their drinks and headed for the exit. He gave them a couple of minutes before he followed them outside. Jim stood in the doorway and watched Harry follow the crowd into another club further down the marina. He waited in the shadows, his eyes glued to the entrance. After an hour or so, the crowd emerged, laughing and larking around as they headed down towards another of the clubs. Harry appeared a few minutes later and watched them disappear inside before making his way down through the marina towards his dinghy, which was moored in the harbour.

Jim followed, and watched as Harry set sail out of the marina, turning east towards Porthleven. He returned to his car in the marina car park and drove away, back to the Lugger Inn. He parked in the shadows just out of sight of the Inn before creeping down the bank to the small boathouse to find Harry's dinghy tied up. He returned to his car, made himself comfortable and settled down for his nightly surveillance.

After many disappointing evenings, Jim once again followed Harry around the clubs and noticed that Harry had taken particular interest in a crowd of the local rich kids, following them from club to club. His heart started to race as he watched the crowd laughing and singing as they staggered down through the marina towards the jetty in the harbour with Harry close behind, keeping in the shadows. 'Could this be the night?' he thought as he tried to stay calm and focused.

Somehow the boys and their girl hangers-on managed to stagger along the jetty and onto a luxury boat without falling into the water. Jim watched as Harry waited till the boat had sailed out of the harbour before jumping into his dinghy and following them, staying back but keeping them in sight. Jim could see they were heading towards Falmouth. He returned to his car and was soon on the road which ran along above the coast. He parked his car in a layby near to Falmouth, which was a perfect vantage point looking onto the coast below. He took out a pair of binoculars and with the help of the bright moonlight he could see the boat, and the dinghy following some way behind. The boat turned off into a small cove but to his surprise and disappointment the dinghy sailed past, turned around and headed back towards Porthleven. Jim turned around and followed Harry, driving carefully on the winding road. The sleepless nights were taking their toll and he struggled to stay alert; he could see Harry was going further and further ahead. He was somewhat relieved when he reached Porthleven.

Harry had tied the dinghy up in the boathouse and run up the hill and into the Inn. He was soon in the cavern and he raised the wall before heading back out of the Inn. But as he was on his way down the hill, he could hear the sound of a car driving up, so he hid in the shadow of the cliff wall and watched as Jim's car flashed by. He waited till he could hear the engine being switched off before running down the hill and into the dinghy and sailing off.

Jim had parked his car amongst the trees at the edge of the car park out of the sight. He had a hot drink from this flask and wrapped a blanket around himself and settled down for the night, waiting hopefully for Harry to come out of the Inn to go back for the boat.

Meanwhile Harry had returned to the cove, picked up the boat and towed it back to the cavern. He lowered the wall.

The next morning, he was in the bar, busy preparing for opening time when George arrived.

'Sorry I'm late,' he said as he started to bottle up.

Harry smiled. 'I'll go and open the doors but I doubt if any of the regulars will be waiting.'

He was most surprised to find Jim and one of the old fishermen standing chatting outside and Jim was surprised and disappointed to see Harry as he followed him into the bar, with Tom the fisherman close behind.

George popped his head above the bar counter and spotted Jim. 'It's a little early for you; has the house burnt down?'

Harry smiled. 'Yes, he does look as though he could use a drink. He looks a little bedraggled. Fill three pints; Tom must be in need of a drink too – it's early for him as well.'

Jim and Tom walked over to their usual seat in the corner of the room and Harry carried the drinks over and sat down beside them.

Tom took a drink and shook his head. 'Have you seen the news? Another boat has gone missing early this morning.'

Jim turned to Harry, who responded quite calmly, 'What?

Another one? You wonder what the police are doing.' He paused a moment to throw a wry smile at Jim. 'No offence, Jim.'

'None taken,' Jim replied, 'but be sure they will catch them, it's only a matter of time.'

Tom shook his head, a huge smirk on his face. 'They laughed at old Henry but he knew what he was talking about.'

Harry chirped in, 'Yeah, Henry and his stories! I believed them while I was growing up but I realise now they were just fantasy.'

Jim detected Harry was a little unnerved by Tom's words. 'What do you mean, Tom?'

Tom took a drink from his glass. 'Henry was convinced there were smugglers' caves in the area, still undiscovered, with tunnels leading up to the churches and inns.' He looked Jim in the eye. 'How else could these boats disappear without trace? They must be hidden in one of those caves and moved on once the search has died down.'

Jim turned to Harry. 'That sounds logical to me; what do you think?'

Harry shuffled uneasily in his seat. 'Fantasy! All the caves have long been discovered and searched over and over again through the years.' He finished his drink before standing up. 'I had better do some work or George will be complaining.' He smiled at Tom before joining George behind the bar.

Jim sank back in his chair with a pensive expression on his face as he turned to Tom.

'I think you are spot on; it's the only logical explanation. I think you deserve a drink.' He stood up and patted Tom on the shoulder. 'I'm so pleased you came in.' He walked over to the bar. 'Can I pay for Tom's next drink, Harry? I think he deserves that. He talks a lot of sense.' He smiled as he made his way out of the bar.

That afternoon, Jim drove his car round to the other side of the cove, overlooking the caves down from the Lugger Inn. He took out a haversack and tent before cautiously climbing down the embankment. He came to a halt when he reached a small cave cut into the embankment. He took off his haversack and tent, placing them inside the cave entrance. He unwrapped the tent and set it up, took out his binoculars from his haversack and crawled into the tent. After making himself comfortable, he focused the binoculars onto the Lugger Inn and scanned down to the boathouse and along the many caves in the cliff face. He smiled to himself; this was the perfect vantage point he needed.

He opened his haversack and took out a sleeping bag, handlamp, primus stove, radio and coffee pot. He set them in place around the tent before crawling out. He zipped up the front flap and climbed back up the embankment.

That evening, he returned with a powerful torchlight. A soft breeze and warm moonlight air caressed his face. He slowly edged his way down the embankment to the cave, filled with a strong feeling of hope, something he had not experienced since his daughter had disappeared. He zipped open the tent and crawled inside. Turning on the handlamp he slipped into his sleeping bag and rolled onto his stomach. Looking through his binoculars, he zoomed in on the boathouse. He could see the back of the dinghy so he set up the primus stove and coffee pot.

Sometime later, he was sitting up drinking a cup of coffee,

looking out of the tent at the calm water below, shimmering like silver beneath the glittering moon, when the stillness of the night was interrupted by the sound of an outboard motor starting up. He quickly put down his cup, rolled over onto his stomach and turned his binoculars towards the boathouse. He watched as the dinghy left the boathouse and set sail up the cove, turning towards Penzance.

He settled back down and picked up a book. As the hours ticked by, he struggled to stay awake; had it not been for several cups of coffee he would surely have nodded off. Outside it was a glorious clear night with a canopy of twinkling stars, and the atmosphere was serene with only the sound of the rippling water below, truly a magical, enchanting experience.

Once again, the spell was broken by the sound of the outboard motor in the distance. He grabbed his binoculars and watched as the dinghy entered the cove and sailed into the boathouse. Jim shook his head – another night of disappointment. He packed up his equipment, crawled out of the tent, zipped up and disappeared back up the embankment.

After several more frustrating evenings, Jim once again made his way down the embankment into his tent and watched Harry sail out of the boathouse and up the cove. Sometime later he watched Harry return but to Jim's amazement Harry sailed straight past the boathouse. Jim slipped out of his sleeping bag to take up a better position to see the dinghy sail further up the cove and disappear into one of caves. His heart was thumping with excitement and, holding the binoculars in one hand and keeping focused on the cave, he picked up his mobile phone and rang Paul at home.

He apologised for waking Paul as he explained the situation. Paul told him not to take any action but to make his way down to the water's edge and Paul would pick him up in the police patrol boat as soon as he could.

Jim was standing on a wooden jetty flashing his torchlight as the patrol boat entered the cove and sailed over to the jetty; Paul stuck out his hand to assist Jim on board and they pushed off. They sailed past the boathouse and slowed down near to the caves. Jim pointed towards the cave. Paul lowered the police dinghy into the water and he and Jim climbed in and entered the cave using Jim's torch for light. Paul steered the dinghy around the cave as Jim moved his torch in every direction. Paul turned to Jim.

'Could it be one of the other caves? They all look the same from outside, more so in the dark.'

Jim shook his head. 'No, I'm one hundred per cent sure this was the one.'

Paul turned the dinghy around. 'He is not here; we can try some of the others close by just to be sure.'

He steered them out of the cave and proceeded to investigate the caves close by but with no joy, and finally they sailed back to the police boat and climbed on board.

Jim was so frustrated. 'I know what I saw. Can we go and search the Inn?'

Paul shook his head. 'Not without a warrant, as well you know. I'm sorry. I realise the dinghy couldn't just vanish but until we have hard evidence, I'm afraid there's nothing we can do.'

They sailed back over to the jetty and Paul dropped Jim

off. He watched as the patrol boat sailed out of the cove before returning to his cave and into his tent, taking up his surveillance position, with his binoculars focused on the cave.

Suddenly, Harry's dinghy, pulling a small lifeboat, sailed out of the cave and turned towards the boathouse. Jim jumped up, punching the air.

'Gotcha at last,' he screamed.

He continued to watch as Harry tied the dinghy up in the boathouse before he steered the lifeboat to the water's edge, tied it up, jumped out and sprinted up the hill towards the Inn. Jim scratched his head, puzzled by what he had witnessed, so he picked up the phone and rang Paul. He explained what had happened and Paul told him to keep watching and report any further events.

He had just hung up when he saw Harry running back down the bank, jumping into the lifeboat and setting sail. He contacted Paul again.

'Keep watching,' Paul told him, 'we have turned around and are on our way back, stay on the phone.'

Jim watched Harry steer the lifeboat into the cave. 'I was right; he has sailed back into that same cave.'

There were a few minutes of silence before Jim jumped up, screaming into the phone. 'You're not going to believe what I'm watching; a luxury boat has just emerged from that very cave we searched.'

'Calm down,' Paul told Jim, 'make your way back down to the water's edge. Keep out of sight but track the direction in which he is heading.'

Jim quickly made his way down to the jetty and flashed

his torchlight as the police launch sped into the cove and over towards him. Paul grabbed Jim's hand and dragged him on board as they sped out of the cove towards the open sea. The crew used their binoculars to scan the open water as they raced ahead at full speed.

Paul used his phone to contact the commander of the French police patrol. 'We are on our way, chasing a possible abduction heading for Benodet.'

'Good news,' the commander replied. 'Now stay out of sight and do not attempt to apprehend or alert the assailants. I will inform Interpol and we will be waiting for you when you enter French waters.'

One of the crew spotted Harry's boat on the horizon. Paul zoomed in through his binoculars as he strode over to the cabin. 'Just keep the boat in your sights; we don't want him to see us,' he said to the man at the helm.

Meanwhile, Harry continued on towards Benodet, unaware of being followed, and finally sailed into the marina. It was early morning and the place was deserted. He tied up as he glanced over and saw Mahmoud stride out of the showroom and head over towards him.

'Any problems?' Mahmoud said as he jumped on board, untied the boat and pushed off the side of the mooring.

Harry shook his head. 'No, it was a calm crossing with no sight of a patrol either side of the Channel,' he replied as he turned the boat around and steered out of the marina.

Paul's police launch continued towards the French coast with Paul still on the phone to the commander, who told him to sail further up the coast, a mile or so away from the Benodet marina, and he would be waiting for them. Paul again scanned the coastline with his binoculars and spotted the French launch in the distance. He turned to the pilot.

'Change course; head up the coast towards that launch in the distance.'

They soon pulled up alongside and the commander jumped on board. He shook Paul's hand.

'Pleased to meet you. My name is Louis. Interpol are tracking the boat; it has just left the marina. We will follow but must keep out of sight, so please join me and my crew and we can move off.'

Paul glanced at Louis. 'Is it okay if Jim tags along? He is the one that has been responsible for solving this mystery.' Louis nodded as he stepped back on board his launch. Paul turned to his crew.

'Turn back to Benodet marina and wait for us there,' he said, as he and Jim followed Louis on board.

Harry and Mahmoud continued up the coast and turned into the inlet and up to the barrier. One of the guards lifted the barrier and they were escorted by the two gunboats up the inlet to the boathouse. Harry and Mahmoud stepped onto the landing area and stood beside an armed guard as four of the crew from the gunship transferred the two girls into their boat.

Suddenly, the sound of a helicopter's rotary blades broke the silence. Harry glanced out of the window to see four helicopter gunships hovering above them. The armed guards grabbed hold of Harry and Mahmoud.

'You have betrayed Hamdan. You will be tortured by him and suffer a slow, painful death.'

The remainder of the guards rushed into the boathouse. 'We are surrounded by armed police and military troops.'

A voice came over a loudspeaker: 'You are totally surrounded and outnumbered; come out with your hands on your heads.'

The two guards holding Harry and Mahmoud pushed them towards the doorway, scanning the area outside. One of the guards turned to the other.

'We must give Hamdan a chance to escape.' He stuck his gun into Harry's back as he pushed him outside. He looked up at the surrounding troops.

'We are coming out with two hostages; we will shoot them unless we are allowed to leave.'

Mahmoud and the other guards followed them out of the boathouse and they slowly made their way over to two parked Range Rovers. All of a sudden one of the military snipers fired his gun and hit the guards holding Harry. The area exploded into a full-scale battle as Hamdan's men opened fire and the military returned fire spraying the guards with a hail of bullets. Harry and Mahmoud cried out as they dropped to the ground with several of the guards. The remainder of the guards threw away their weapons and raised their hands in the air.

The military troops quickly moved in. They removed the weapons and tied up the prisoners. One of the troopers checked Harry's pulse and shook his head, before rolling Mahmoud over but again there was no sign of life. They loaded the prisoners onto one of the four army trucks before they sped off up the tarmac road.

When they reached the electronic gates, one of the troopers dragged one of the prisoners off the truck and, holding a gun to his head, forced him to operate the control to open the gates. They continued along the tree-lined driveway, Paul and Jim following behind in a police Land Rover. Four helicopter gunships hovered above the château as the army trucks took up their positions in a line in front of the château. The troops, in full combat dress, jumped out of the trucks and took cover behind the trucks, their weapons trained towards the entrance. The police Land Rover pulled up some 200 metres further back.

The commander of the troops lifted up a loud speaker. 'Throw your weapons out and walk out with your hands raised.'

He waited a few minutes before repeating the demands. Still no response. He contacted one of the helicopters and it responded, swooping down and blasting the front doors with a rocket. The commander waved his troops forward. They threw several phosphorus grenades towards the entrance to cover their charge as they zigzagged their way up to the entrance and flooded through.

The Land Rover moved up to the trucks. Paul and Jim slipped out, took up position behind the trucks and watched as the sound of gunfire echoed around the château. The exchange of fire continued for some time before slowly subsiding into silence and the troops emerged with Hamdan and his men, their hands tied behind their backs.

Paul and Jim strode up to the commander.

'Is it safe to enter?' Jim asked.

He nodded his head. 'Yes, but two of the troopers and I will escort you,' he replied as he led them inside.

They cautiously entered the hallway with Paul and Jim close

behind, their heads moving in all directions as they scanned the reception area and the staircase to the first floor. They searched the ground floor room by room before the commander led them up the staircase onto the landing, making sure they checked each room on the first floor, scouring cupboards, wardrobes and dressing areas.

With no luck they returned to the ground floor and Jim discovered a door under the stairs, camouflaged in the oak-panelled passageway. Jim tried the door; it was locked. One of the troopers used the butt of his rifle to hammer the lock several times before the two troopers used their shoulders to burst the door open. Guns cocked, the two troopers led the group down a staircase and into a large cellar, which contained rows of racks, stocked with bottles of wine and spirits. Jim tapped on the wall as he worked his way around the cellar.

'There must be another room,' Paul joined in, sounding every inch of the walls.

The Commander rubbed his chin. 'Maybe there is another room off one of the other rooms,' he said, as he made his way out of the cellar and up the stairs.

The others followed him. Jim trailed behind and, all of a sudden, he dropped to his knees.

'Wait! I think I've found some sort of hatch.'

Paul rushed back into the cellar. Cleverly disguised as part of the floor behind the door was a large ring-pull. Jim and Paul grabbed hold and, with an almighty heave, lifted up the hatch to reveal a flight of stairs.

The Commander and his troopers rushed back in to see Jim as he disappeared down the stairs.

'Come back, Jim,' the Commander shouted, 'we need to search the area. There could be gunmen down there.'

But Jim was using his shoulder to try and break down the door at the bottom of the stairs. The troopers quickly joined Jim and used their rifle butts to burst open the door, revealing six young girls huddled together in the corner of a dimly lit room.

Jim called out his daughter's name. 'Jackie – Jackie is that you?'

One of the girls staggered to her feet. 'Father,' she screamed as she put out her arms, tears flooding down her face.

Jim ran over, lifted her up in his arms and said, 'I thought I'd never see you again,' as he no longer held his emotions and the tears just flowed. Jackie was sobbing uncontrollably.

'You have come just in time.' She wiped her eyes. 'One of the guards told us that a boat that would take us to Algeria had docked this morning.'

Jim took off his jacket and placed it around her shoulders as he led her out of the room, hugging her tightly. Paul, the Commander and his troopers helped the other girls to their feet and escorted them up the stairs.

When they left the château, Hamdan and his men were being herded into a police van. Jim scowled over at Hamdan. Paul led the other girls over to join Jim and his daughter.

Jim shook his head as he glared over at Hamdan. 'How could anyone do this to innocent young girls? What would have happened to them in Algeria?' He shook his head. 'Best not think about that but the white slave trade is still going on in different parts of the world, young people being sold into slavery.' He turned to Paul. 'What about Harry?'

Paul shook his head. 'He's dead; shot by one of Hamdan's men.'

'Why?' said Jim. 'What made him change? He was such a quiet, likeable young man from a respectable family. His parents will be horrified by his actions and devastated by his death.'

'So sad,' replied Paul. 'We should take the girls to hospital to be checked over and cleaned up,' as he ushered them over to a waiting ambulance.

Jim helped Jackie into the ambulance. 'We will follow in the police vehicle and join you at the hospital.'

The ambulance drove off, Jim and Paul climbed into the police Range Rover and followed close behind, down the drive.

The following day, back at the Lugger Inn, George escorted Paul, Jim, John and Mary down the tunnel and into the cavern. As he switched on the lights, they stood open-mouthed, dumbstruck by the sight before them. Paul scratched his head.

'No wonder they couldn't track the stolen boats. Harry must have brought them straight into the cavern and dropped the wall. The coast guards and police patrols could never find a trace.'

Jim shook his head, totally bewildered. 'I actually saw Harry enter the cave but still couldn't discover the secret after searching the cave.'

George glanced over to John. 'It was one thing stealing the boats, but the girls – that's another level of crime. What happened to him to change him so dramatically?'

Mary began to sob and John put his arm around her. 'We are both so ashamed of what he did but we think it had something to do with the death of his beloved grandfather

Henry; after that he changed completely.' He pondered for a moment before he continued, 'The air rescue teams were all tied up as they answered SOS calls from the party-going rich kids, leaving Harry to try and save his grandfather by himself. At first, he blamed himself; then all of his anger, frustration and hatred was focused on those kids.'

Mary wiped her eyes as she looked around the cavern. 'After Henry's death, Harry seemed to slip into a fantasy world. His grandfather's stories of pirates and smugglers, the haunted dreams and finally the regression into a past life made him believe he was as his grandfather had told him; he was a pirate in that past life.' She took a deep breath as she scanned the area. 'The discovery of this cavern must have been the final piece of the jigsaw and somehow, Harry felt it was inevitable that he take up that role and at the same time avenge the death of his beloved grandfather.'

Paul nodded in agreement. 'We will never know the truth but it would seem Mary could be right.' He turned to John. 'What are your plans for the cavern?'

John turned to Mary. 'We have not made up our minds yet but we have a few ideas. As the Inn is a tourist attraction through its links with smugglers, the obvious thing would be to open it up to the public.'

As they turned to leave, John smiled. 'Old Henry would have been in his element showing people the proof of his stories and no doubt would have made up a host of new ones.' John ushered them out of the cavern and turned off the lights.

Harry's spirit appeared in the cavern. Standing on the landing area, he glanced about.

'Are you there, Grandfather?' he said in a soft voice. There was a moment of silence before his grandfather's voice whispered, 'Over here, Harry, over here.'

Harry turned to see his grandfather float out of the tunnel, followed by several pirates and smugglers. Harry floated over to join them and they disappeared back up the tunnel.